Also by Eve Shelnutt:

The Love Child (1979)
The Formal Voice (1982)

EVE SHELNUTT

THE
FORMAL
VOICE

BLACK SPARROW PRESS

SANTA BARBARA
1982

ACKNOWLEDGEMENT

Grateful acknowledgement is given to the editors of the following periodicals where some of these stories originally appeared: *Agni Review*, *Black Warrior Review*, *Carolina Quarterly*, *Denver Quarterly Review*, *Great Lakes Review*, *The Literary Review*, *Palaemon Press*, *Ploughshares*, *Quarterly West*, *Slow Loris Reader*, *Story Quarterly*, and *West Branch*.

LIBRARY OF CONGRESS CATALOGING IN PUBLICATION DATA

Shelnutt, Eve, 1943-
  The formal voice.

  I. Title.
PS3569.H39363F6   813'.54   82-4183
ISBN 0-87685-549-4   AACR2
ISBN 0-87685-548-6 (pbk.)
ISBN 0-87685-550-8 (signed cloth ed.)

to Mark Shelton

So far beyond the casual solitudes. . . .
—*Wallace Stevens*

TABLE OF CONTENTS

THE FORMAL VOICE

Driving with "Raoul"

*She wanted nothing he could not bring her
by coming alone.* —Wallace Stevens

ALREADY WE HAD MADE LOVE three times in a room where the
mattress slid to the floor and the color of the bathroom was the
aqua of peacocks. And by then he had shown me the pictures of
his grandmother, beautiful under the portico, high on a hill, her
hair swept back by wind he described as coming from the river for
her pleasure, for her pleasure inside the house the tray of pewter,
the crystal bowl of roses. She was slim and her eyes so unwavering
they broke her men like colts. Her men, said Raoul, never got
what they wanted, were not once fulsome.

So she is not real.

Raoul is lovely. His teeth in the morning sun are almost
translucent, tiny splinters of cracked ice. His tongue almost
black—*Ah, Senorita, look at that, a great bird flying through our room
and you missed it. Hear me sigh.*

Then he was driving and sighing (a sigh so deep I pictured his
insides, as he wanted), one hand on my knees, the right hand,
which he lifted to point to all the houses of all the girls he had
had, yellow houses inside of which the girls lie split on couches,
and their mothers retire to paint their own bedrooms lilac.

"We should have met before, Raoul."

His black fur curls. *Sadness* (he says it as my name): *You are
about to tread on territory no one can touch without being sad. Do not do
it. I will kill you if you do it.*

13

And I loved Raoul most of all as we drove, behind us on the car seat his books of poems, their leaves fluttering in the wind of the cracked glass. Raoul would crawl into the obelisk of his work, the person of his contrived salvation, read from those books—*after* we passed the yellow houses, after he untied my bones again. *Do not think*, he says, his teeth saw-tight, and I go through them: Little Willow.

So I tell him about my boots, how they are black as black widows and how I wear them below a skirt so short my fuschia panties show. I walk in where Raoul is eating ham and eggs and western toast with raspberry jam, I sit facing him a booth away, I stick one toe into the aisle and I begin to paint my nails magenta, humming, cocking my head this way and that. I eat as if I may starve, so Raoul follows me to my room, follows the clicking of the high-heeled boots on the tile floor, and when he has undone me he leans above me on one elbow and says, *Do not spoil nothing by saying its name, which I tell you* (he strokes my wet brow) *as the Grandee of all Grandees, yes?*

Sweetness, he says, whispering at the 40-mile marker, *I am once again—ah yes—tumescent. Consider it.*

And the car is consuming valleys, the sky blues, my ribs lace, lace, the complements of lace. . . . Gun it, Raoul, I say, to which he slows down to a cart's pace, speeds, slows, speeds. . . . And in a room, high up, with a view of Raoul's mountains, throws me on the bed, draws back the curtains until all the sun is with us, one perfect circle a jewel on my belly. *So now I will have you.* He climbs on.

Of course I know his real name, do not want it, in the room where he reads, crawl into rosewood and tapestry to listen like a silken thread, one of a leaf, perpetuity of leaves—his voice so fine he would leave it to sons, and he *has* sons, pewter, roses, a woman under the portico because of whom he chafes alone in the boat-house by the endless river. Hear me sigh.

The ladies ask questions, unfolding the parchment of their foreheads as if *this* were his career, fleshless ache of words I have, since Raoul, in clear perspective, my skin maleable even under chandeliers. I hike my skirt, he looks past the woman in flamingo knits, and soon, soon we are sleeping our sleep.

And every morning in each new town, he lifts me high in his arms, cape billowing against the imagined banisters, carries me down to eat because *My Hidalgo, we must keep up our strength—very important. His* forehead mirror-smooth, above it the blackest brows and hair. How long have we been *doing* this? Outside one room the cleaning ladies listened, and Raoul laughed rhythmically for them all the while. They felt his body swoop.

Each day we drove deeper into the state, toward red clay, squat trees, hints of moss, idle men draped on benches, and they turned to watch us, sniffing the air, and, surely, had Raoul left me for a minute they would have taken me, in heat, there by the bright blue trash·barrels, the sun and their looking an extra layer of clothing. We began to suffocate. And the food was bad; flies rested on the Danish pastry; beds covered in pale yellow chenille; and his audiences languid but not satisfied—ever in the lives of their skin—his voice the only voice. Mornings we drank whiskey and water; and all the women were fat. I said, "Raoul, didn't you *ever* manage to get down here?" And he said, *Basta.* Growing mean.

There were pictures I could have shown him: my father in a jacket of navy velvet before a Cadillac and its ornament of lifted wings and, behind the tail fins, the host of beautiful women whose images an imprint on him made the solitary woman meeting him imagine herself alone with him in the hooded car, miles of driving. Or Peter, whose eyes Raoul would have recognized, the fraternity of absolute perception, and the wish to look away.

In rooms so small we began to hate each other's silver-handled brushes laid out on plastic counters, I almost asked, "Who *are* you?" But I knew. *Now*, Raoul said, taking me.

My mother is last seen washing in the river. When she looks up, her eyes hold surprise, wild with longing, presentiment of death. So I leave her, because even her he might have taken in without crying; he owns all the Parisienne ponies on a hill.

Then, miles from anywhere, in a dream, tiny Misha comes wafting in as Raoul lies sleeping. It was as if we had left the transom open, it was as if we were among the chosen. For Raoul woke saying, "Misha." Imaginary friend of his first-born, the most-loved. And Raoul's boy is *in* the room; I am not dressed.

After that, he *talked.* Not "Raoul." "Please call for Raoul," I would ask him as we drove. "We need him." But, I learned, Raoul was out of town, each town, girls rocking gently on their porches, waving us by—commonfolk, and doomed.

A lovely voice modulates precisely what one does not want to hear. *It* is contrivance, artifact: I learned from how I ached. (My mother is smiling wryly now.) I read his books to myself, in my own voice—flat—a flogging.

On the edge of country we recognized, he read one last time—that night himself and Raoul *in a single body.* He became, without warning, the one civilized man, perfect words and, in Raoul, the perfect body of the words. We are not ready for such intimacy; it sears.

"You frightened me," I said from the floor of our room where I had dropped, the only time, in weariness. And one last time Raoul lifted me up, carrying me across the room, saying it was a bountiful room, two beds and a shower to sing in, singing.

Misha, you are innocent, you did not know what you were doing. It is, I do understand, so very enticing to be innocent.

After that, we wrote to one another. Sometimes I would undress and, holding the phone, touch myself, as he told me. And once I sent in the mail my black satin dress, which he held next to him, sent back: *no.* In his boys' rooms, the clothes are neatly folded; in his study, the books are bound in leather. There is space enough to drown in.

He suffered.

But does Raoul *know* what is required to be taken? The moon, My Exquisite Lover, is the emblem of death, light of everything left over, the world: conglomerate wolf, baying: *Come down* for an aperitif by the fire, sleep under ironed sheets, and, in your place, we will position our women under the portico.

And I would have been one of those women, given half a chance, oh yes, because the moon is colder still.

Imagine, instead, a car which holds my mother, father, and me. For a long time, I look outside, at the countryside, at how the people live on enchantment. Then, like Misha, I turn to the room inside: What's going on here? A coming-home to get born.

In a car, nothing happens that is not human, so small, nothing larger than human. Its motion the rhythm of desire, and, my father said, Why not just drive? Knowing the body is never satisfied and cannot, anyway, rest. Each night, crossing America, the moon is in a different place. He loved the driving. He rested one hand on my mother's thigh, sometimes I saw it crawl between her legs. For several years, she hummed.

And she would have been the perfect woman for Raoul except she heard *her* father's voice (ordinary, and kind) saying, *"Settle,"* until, rib by rib, she broke, my father trading tires and gassing up.

Too late I whisper to The Woman Washing in the River: anyone who loves is the perfect iconoclast, keeping the world away, one window-pane away, and the fruitless baying is muted. Now she is in one place and the telephone rings, which she answers wet with longing for any flamboyant thing, and, on the other end, a man is selling carpets.

And, driving with my father, he tells me of his women and points to their houses, yellow in the dusk. He doesn't own a thing but singing and somewhere, surely, my mother's breaking, lodged like an orb. But, then, he never tried, not once, to be The Civilized Man: world and body one. It is not time, Raoul, who, oh sadness, traded in disorder, one wife for yet another, and dreams of Misha's falsetto voice.

And *if* I dream of my father the incestuous dream, having heard so much in the one small room, it is because I am the willed daughter—love makes one choose order *or* the person and, to love, I took him in. I am the perfect embodiment of Daughter: *flesh of my flesh*.

Raoul, I say to myself, what did I care of your earthly discretions, order and the chaos of your black mind curling? When the phone rings, I see you in the sunset, red cape across the back of your horse, sunset burning. You lift one hand, and wave.

We love as many as we can manage and, truly, I try to think the girls rocking on the porches are only resting up. *I am rested up.* Should you ride in one day, teeth ablaze and open, saying a great bird is flying through the sky, do not miss it, I think. . . .

I think, after that, if Raoul says one word, even the words of enchantment which I once loved, I will kill him, no?

The Idea of Order

IN ANOTHER TIME (Annie imagines), by the sea, where blue cornflowers grew even in the sand, she would have been able, wedged in the camouflage of blood relations, to stand at the water's edge, waving and waving, an ankle-length apron lifting between her arms like drying laundry so that he, rowing outward from which tossed plain it was accepted he might not return, could look up, see her, and smile to himself, the wholly impure (his wife and children themselves as stalk of cornflower on the far rise) made pure by death's proximity, that leveler, past the red tide. All women made melancholy, the extant marriage-of-marriages, the only difference (she would cross herself) who got him, if the little boat brought them back to be got, by the slab table holding his pot of black tea. Then, you could look under the table and count the pairs of shoes and wool stockings, notice the gradations in size, believe the floor was wearing down from years of such scraping, the dog in the middle of so many feet as if the feet were warming on the russet fur. And that, if you were waiting, might be an enormous difference, against which his noticing once the bright blue veins along your wrists or the almost imperceptible pause in your walk when you saw him passing might be as nothing. He might, after all, fall asleep at the table, forgetful in bone-weariness, as if death were practicing.

19

As it is, no one in his immediate family is dying, or especially abject—time harpooned—so he fires up the Chevy Nova and is down the road into a web of falling leaves, yellow, the astringent color. Then he speeds, daydreaming, and the police stop him, flipping the ticket, after which ceremony of the blue raceme he takes off again daunted, with, now, a future cash-flow problem, and the gas gauge is on near-empty, with the possibility of a tire blow-out, retreads close to flapping, her face before him like a stop sign or, simply, *caution* as, in this waiting-time, she imagines sirens and converging life-support units and the high-pressure hose. Her face burns on the cold window pane, the left cheek grazed: she *needs* him. And he has not said *when* he is coming or if he might come again.

Which waiting—portent—was like her mother's, though they were married (she slides, does Annie, indignant, into the white wicker chair by the frosted window: why ferret the whirr of desire?), in that time of the war when it was known one helped, as he (*Father:* the quick look around the breakfast table to see no one is ill), while she knitted, wrapped, kissed the two girls quickly in that fever of giving aid, swung his body from one side of New York City to another, to broadcast vignettes of sorrow-and-bearing-up, before all hearts were felled by the photographs of thin bodies behind chain link fencing, neither male nor female, nor human but in the curled fingers on the metal webbing and in the rapt attention of the eyes to sights which made words frivolous: *lampshade, gold filling, eye glass, box car,* the single severed beribboned braid found by a Russian prisoner, belonging, though he wouldn't know, to a girl who had once lived in Rostock.

So, married? He began, after that, moving them across America, Annie's mother, initially, raising, merely, the left eyebrow, as if to ask, Are you sure? And Annie, then no higher than the table's edge, saw her mother stopped in time in the house off Long Island Sound, in its dining room where light came from two windows.

One window faced the street over which trees hung their branches, muting light; the other, taller, receiving all the afternoon sun, which cut into the rose leaf rug and the mahogany table covered with the linen cloth where sat the silver bowls and shakers, the vase of flowers. Across from the table stood the cabinet where she stored what was delicious (and only much later told of how her feet swelled as she waited in line for sugar, which did not change *this* picture). She hears in the distance the whistle of the commuter train, envisions the rack of bicycles waiting, and knows that he is coming. She stands before the cabinet, in half-light, lifts one hand, then rests it on the plate of fudge.

It is to Annie, in memory, a *tableau vivant,* never repeated, repeatable, spoken of, or, but by her, remembered. Except: the wrist of any person is the fragile body part and, because—only because!—it is higher up, the inside of the elbow the place where one ought to be kissed.

Later, she supposes, they ate the fudge, the light moved away no slower than usual.

Air and salt, air and salt.

It could *snow,* says Annie, before he gets here, which timing only *he* knows, the afternoon light coming over his left shoulder as he drives, making of the right hand which holds the wheel a shadow on the red vinyl seat covers where a passenger might be on another day, the history which drives him to her like that shadow and, too, wordless. In how a hand moves on a wheel, or how a woman can touch her ribs while talking, or a sister's shoulders curve, or the hand reaching up to touch the place where hair *had* been: *there* is history, binding.

Her father drove and drove. He said once, when she was five, "Annie, why are you always so hot?" and stopped in Tucson to buy a basin, a stopper, and filled it with water to set her in, saying, "Now hush," and it became clear, in his voice lowering and in the manner he closed car doors, this road was the place they were driving to *get* to, no matter the road changed, nor the terrain beyond, nor the seasons, the years, the gradations of light, the make of car, or the sizes of the two girls in the back seat. So what one watched was the *play* of light (eight fragile bluing wrists!), and what one listened for was changes in breathing. And of the skin of those one loved. . . .

He laughed, his laughing said: *this is it,* and *loosen up.*

What makes a woman eligible? When the down of her skin stands up, when the teeth itch, and the eyes narrow, for seeing shape within shape, as watching a boat when there is no timing to indicate when the eye began to remember his body, which before it saw.

The inheritance spent, he went off to work, a side-trip, and, as if it had been yesterday, he drove up months later and, walking into the rented house, any state, slapped his back pocket, saying, "So let's *go,* Sweets."

"Where *to?*"

Annie remembers her mother's voice as always split, half-wedded to his motion, to the sway of his body out and around any obstacle (as a car, he said, seemed to *become* animal, swerving on highways away from animals born indecisive in the age of highways), the *jauntiness* of it, the other half of that voice. . . .

Annie's sister Cynthia is, in the car, stolid flesh. If she looked up from her book, in her eyes such hatred showed it was a room she bunkered in. Beautiful, but who would *know* it? And what was Cynthia waiting *for*? If she spoke, it was to say such things as, "We had a *pond* behind that house. I bet you didn't even know that. We could have *skated* on it."

"We don't *have* skates," Annie would whisper.

"*Stupid*," Cynthia would say. "Like *him*," rolling her eyes.

So her mother's voice in the quavering-half was (*only* perhaps) remembering imagined delights, as, it was possible to think, she anticipated in the mind's eye all the pretty flowers printed on all the material, and their matching threads, the buttons, all the pictures of thin girls posing in the pattern books that day, when she was sixteen, she and her mother were walking hand-in-hand to the store. And out of nowhere came the car, speeding and swerving, swiping from her hand her mother, dragging the body almost to the store they had been going toward. And then Annie's mother, formerly sleepy in the body's age of shoring up for love, was eligible; it showed in how she moved. But even Annie could envision how the sun had warmed them as they walked in the late afternoon, and hear the murmuring of their voices as they talked about flounces and bows and what color for such innocence.

The bodies of those you love, says Annie to herself, her nose pressing on the glass as she stands to look out, are as your own; they ache, want out, can't *get* out.

And so my father drove.

It was not often she and Cynthia went visiting outside the various houses; it could be Cynthia never stepped into a stranger's house until she grew up and began making so many friends with whom she laughed so loudly and said so many frivolous things *she* seemed a stranger. But that was *after* the idea of order (*Imposter*! and *But for memory we four are aliens now and our eyes burn at the sight*) and Annie, it is true, hadn't known of the pond, the set of swings, the baby down the block born with two rows of teeth complete. Once she went inside the house across the road (Florida?—natural heat the curved flame of memory)—went in because the old man asking her in looked like her father's father and she missed them both. There, in the little side room lay his wife on a day bed; he said, "She can't talk but she can see all right." Which was why he had made the porch himself, and set in all the walls jalousied windows, and planted pines on two sides. The light was like that light in the house on Long Island Sound, and the wife's hand rested on the cover's top—when Annie stepped close, it lifted, the fingers curled, the sun caught in the stone of the ring, and the veins showed through the almost translucent skin. From far off came a train, and, from that distance, the whistle. Their dog lay sleeping at the foot of the bed, its fur russet. And because it was late autumn, you could feel the light change and the coolness coming down as if a sheet. He reached to pull her covers up, and then you could hear her snoring, a faint ruffle in the thin chest, breath which could not possibly reach the toes, and it seemed to Annie she could see them bluing under the plaid cover. Her lashes long, like a young girl's, and black, startling on the white skin. He loved her; and the room seemed as small as the inside of a car.

Then the breaking up, as under a wave, though it was inland: Orlando, Florida. "*Lord*, what a place," Annie's mother said, enduring the heat added to the heat of waiting. "Across the street they're putting up a fast-food joint, yet, and you girls'll be *over* there if I don't watch," not knowing the settling-in she was about to propose contained precisely such establishments—and the crinkle of crinoline slips, the inch-thick ankle socks, boys who asked you to wear their rabbits' feet on a neck chain, all of which Cynthia did in a flash of melting: my sister, ha!, Annie would say as her mother fretted in the new house, in and out of the house fretting and, by this, embracing the world.

"We're leaving him, is what *I* say."

That day, Annie remembers, everything they owned stood out in the bright Florida sunshine; no rug, she sat on the floor, cooling, and, from that perspective, saw best the feet of the round table, her mother's back bent over a cardboard box, the porcelain teapot making a shadow on the wood floor. And for the first time she realized that what *he* owned was always with him in the car, not even a sash of a robe among the belongings on the floor.

During the trip (*"Home,"* said Annie's mother, meaning among blood relations none of them remembered), the trailer welded to the used car broke apart, all they had packed scattered on a mountain road. Annie's mother said it was a "nuisance," and she sighed. Sighing, she rested her forehead on the steering wheel, then softly whimpered—the only time—and Cynthia leaned forward to say, "For pity's sakes, don't do *that.*" Annie hated her. *Would* he look them up now and then?

Into the permanent house, strangers came. "Make some friends!" and "Join something, some after-school club, or something," said Annie's mother.

But she didn't know how. And when he did come to check up on the girls, only Annie was able to remember what had become of the unabridged dictionary: "Got to have it, Sweets," he said. "Might need to look something up, you know?"

She told him it went down the mountain-side, halfway between Asheville and Hendersonville. "It's probably still there," she said, "I saw it sliding but I couldn't get it; it was all a mess."

He rubbed her head, he said (softly), "Well, you know your mother. Brace up." And when he left—his hand on the door-frame, the Bulova watch gold as ever, and the hair on his hand black as it had been—it was the last intimate gesture of a child-hood.

Then Annie hears the Chevy Nova spinning in, the sound of leaves under the tires, and the door slamming as she rises, stiff and sleepy. Touching her chest, she feels her heart beating, as it always races when he visits—he notices, reaching over when they are almost asleep to touch that place, as if to say *goodnight* though it is always afternoon, the stolen hours. And, before she sleeps, what she sees last is the shape of his hand. The subsuming sight.

And, at the door, they have nothing to say *for* themselves, unsanctified but in how bodies incline, nor would she know *how* to ask if she is happy, this highest passion (as Cynthia, embracing the world, would say) so absolutely questionable.

Except, as he holds her, she imagines his car outside dismantling at once, spontaneous combustion; she laughs, and, in the room, in such expanse as they encompass breathing, is, she thinks, the smell of salt air, and the room itself a boat, miles off-shore.

The Pilot-Messenger

To dream with one eye open. . . .
—Santayana

SOMETIMES THE THREE OF THEM would awaken simultaneously and lie still under the piqué coverlets, watching the light seep through the curtains until they were suffused. Or close their eyes against the light, remembering and reinventing. There was, of course, no way to prove the times of their bodies had caught them at once in this combustion of waking, the mother and father in one bed set apart from the girl by a thin wall covered in roses and half-moons of ochre. Nor proof that they also imagined bodies unlike their own in repose against the white, white sheets— longer legs and toes uncurled, skin smooth as marble-table tops, pores tight, and breathing that would go on forever.

They were ordinary, so ordinary who would notice?, the question itself a bodiless heartbeat.

But, those rare times, they listened for the same sounds, which came in flat country across miles—wind in the grasses and the weeds such as Queen Anne's lace, dogs foraging in the wood's recesses, and the train bound for Atlanta. Behind the house sat their trailer, its hitch covered in clover, and, if a wind were high, there would be, too, the sound of the tarpaulin flapping against the wooden slats.

Then, their own impatience, rising. "Are you awake?", they called to one another, as if the tiny house had numberless rooms where one of them might be lost.

27

In the interval between the asking and a slow lifting of "yes" in the three voices, so different—the father's cleaned of any accent and the girl's too soft—it seemed, then, time has stopped and that there was among them a fourth person, lodged invisibly inside them, and moving. Air, around the veins and weaving through the little coveys where muscles bunched.

The curtains moved in the morning breeze—whitecaps on the bottomless day—and the light began to make the four rooms appear shabby, a mistake occurring before them. The birds set against one another in cacaphony. So the three would get up, begin, their bodies closing, as the roof of a child's doll house, the miniature brass hinges disappearing. And, at once, this semblance of air inside them would take his own sleep, no longer alluded to in the hot desolation of three people waking at once.

The girl dressed herself, in pinafores on whose thin straps grew ruffles as if on her arms butterflies. She wrapped the sashes tight so that, with time, the waist caved in—the first of shapeliness, where sand falls through.

Her father watched her leave, dressed like this for the outer world, as if by her body's timing he judged his own. He wouldn't work—"Shit no, unless I get a connection," which meant Florida, where, in his mind's eye, flamingoes stood always one-legged before a backdrop of sunset. Or New York: incalculable. Then—would he take them along? I expect not, his eyes said, surveying.

But maybe *she* would be wholly beautiful. He would move himself, her body a current, and his own death a lighthouse above them. So he fooled time, sat in the blue-covered chair, smoked, watched the yellow bus disappearing in the dust. *Annie.*

Who chewed her hair in sleep. If you came upon her dreaming, you might see her teeth loosen it, and the ends of the braids would lie flat on the pillow-slip, which dampened. He had felt the spot. Slowly, the ends of the braids would curl. Sometimes she cried out; he would touch her, as if to enter the dream. He loved her; and she would not turn out entirely beautiful. Her face would move with every thought and, in time, only the thoughtful would watch her go by on a street. *If* she could be opened, then what?

He would sit by her, thinking. When it was hot, he fanned the air between them.

What did the mother know of this formal setting, her daughter's youth the damask cloth whereon would one day sit the silver shakers, goblets, and the tiny swans of salt? Or, knowing, think? Really, there was nothing to think. And often the father would lean above his wife, head resting in the palm of one hand, the elbow making an eddy of darkness in the pillow. He would watch the curving cheek or the spread of her lashes, the beautiful parts. Sometimes *she* would cry out, and then listen to his breath hold. So what were words.

Yet, often, at the school where she taught, when the children were outside eating from lunchpails under the chinaberry trees, she stood looking out past these trees, still and with one hand held waist-high, as if she were just stepping forward. She would stand this way for minutes, and in the heat of the sky where she was looking was nothing at all. She seemed almost weightless, and the sun shone through the plaid dress so that the shape of her body was visible.

She doesn't eat, and when the children return, she looks up, startled, recalling them. The children like her because they are not everything to her and what interests her is a mystery. Where did she come from and where is she going? To tease her from absorption, they ask her this. Her hands fan out, she smiles as if embarrassed, she is almost pretty, and she says, "Oh, lots of places," lifting her eyes coquettishly, until they think London, Paris, the state capital. Her bones seem to rub against each other, *place* the angle of his blue chair, in any house, and the girl moving between them, and the times of waking together: Pauline, Annie, him (the sleeper), and the pilot-messenger wanting the broad daylight.

Miles from Pauline's school, to the east, sits Annie's school made of concrete blocks, the long, low corridors jutting this way and that as if it had been the architect's passion to cover all pasture-land. After months, still the building frightens Annie. Once in her desk, she presses her body to its chair and feels her smallness as reassuring. In the room, she is silent, but, to be polite, as Pauline has taught her, she keeps her eyes on the teacher's face, and all of her teachers have thought her studious when, in fact, she is dreaming.

At recess, sometimes a girl will inch up to Annie and ask, "What does your daddy do?", as she pictures her own father in the work shirts of forest green, wisps of cotton clinging to the collar, the white tee-shirt edging up on the adam's apple. "T.V.," says Annie. "Sometimes he's on T.V." And the girl will say, cocking her head, "I bet I saw him on The Edge of Night when I was sick. Was he on The Edge of Night?" Annie will look away, lifting a wing of her pinafore as the girl says, "I bet he was."

When Annie runs home, always running!, and sees him in the afternoon light coming over his left shoulder, one leg crossed and the Camel held near the left knee, the hand still and the smoke blue as the filament of dragonflies, she will think anything is possible.

So she read, everything they wouldn't ask at school, this knowledge wordless as the air between them in the house. "You," he would often declare at dinner, pointing a fork or a half-piece of the white bread, "are a bundle."

"*Am* I?" she would ask, seeing her mother's head tilt their way and her fork hold.

And he would say, solemnly, "Yes."

Then Pauline would giggle: "Crazy, I swear," getting up with the plates and shaking her head over them, her two wonders, while he would wink, try to slap her fanny as she passed.

So anything could happen. *Echo, appendages, walking stick, the icy mountains of China.* Could I ask you anything I wanted, in the whole wide world? He would say, Why sure, Sweets, ask away.

A presumption, as the use of feet or a hollow at the collarbone: he moved them here and there, to acquire such knowledge, sensing. "You two pack what you have to, the precious stuff, and don't dilly-dally around." As if suddenly starved. And Pauline watching him, Annie's eyes on her: What's all over you, Honey (let me tell you), you don't have to understand. Music, down the spine.

"You drive." Pauline drove.

Annie would turn all the way around in the car seat to look at the house—growing smaller.

Traveling, those long days and nights longer still, there was no (proofless) waking together, the car air and the air in the two-bit motels stale. They would grow silent, he would have to remind them: "Perk up for Christ's sakes and pass the bag with the sardines."

Annie worried, a debauche in the area of the stomach. Pauline would understand, but she was listening, elsewhere. And thus Pauline annointed each new house, tilting her head, stilling it anew, as though the house were a shell from a beach on which he had landed them. All schools, Annie learned, were the same. Sometimes they left the cows out in the back where the cheerleaders got to park their cars. Most houses had roses twining up the walls. They didn't own a T.V. set. *Who* was missing?

He didn't die; he began to corner Pauline in the kitchen, by the open refrigerator, and say to her, "I got an idea." Then there would be no sound at all from the kitchen, and was he, then, touching her?

The screen door slamming behind her, hyacinth bushes hitting her face, mouth a gill, as a fish's when beached—Annie ran. Found, on her own, a boy—whose hair was yellow curls; on his arms, tiny ringlets; where she put her hand on his shirtless back, nothing at all but the coolness of water, *her* secret, as he touched her nose and her shoulder bones under the pinafore.

He was nobody, he was Curtis Johnson Junior, who on weekdays delivered the *Belton Express* on a Schwinn painted silver; and none of her men, ever, would be anybody at all, the cool absence, anything possible if only they didn't talk.

Some nights, still, the father would watch her in sleep, placing his own hand along the bridge of her nose where one blue vein surfaced, feeling with the other hand the boniness of a knee or the calf-muscles bunched, sore. He wanted off scot-free. Every god-damn house has a leaky faucet in it somewhere, you know that? he told Pauline, easing into her and holding one of her arms tight against the pillow, another under her as she thinned.

Finally he wanted luxury. It might be a vase he saw in a window in Charleston as they walked after eating the peck of raw oysters near the Battery. Or the juice-squeezer he won as a door prize at the auctions in Hendersonville, where the fattest twins in the world rode their motorcycles on Main Street. A second-hand harp, for Annie, his watching her as she picked out a song almost Oriental: a picture he placed himself in as though to lend perspective. Pauline cooked, rolling her eyes heavenward, for herself, and waited.

Often, when night came, it seemed they were the same as they had always been, Pauline sewing under the brass lamp and his head thrown back against the blue chair as his eyes shut and the Max Brand western dangled from a finger, and Annie not listening for the sound of a bicycle on the gravel. Light soft in the room, water, somewhere, dripping, and heat as a presence.

Pauline would hum, and when she held up against Annie the dress, with long, tight sleeves, on which she had been sewing, she would say, "Well!," standing back, looking with her eyes narrowed and the mouth a half-curve, a benediction. Annie could feel in that instant a mouth on the back of her neck or along the inside of an arm, the coolest spot. Soon they would all. . . .

But she didn't know. And when he was watching her in sleep, when the light was diffuse in the grass and there was no sound in the house, not even Pauline's even breathing, nor wind coming from any place, and his tie loosened at the neck and dangling between his knees as he sat curved toward her—then, if she asked him anything at all, he wouldn't answer, no.

Before they moved, his closet bloomed with shirts of green, the palest blue, and yellow of dyed eggs, with the pins of the wrappings still stuck in the collars or holding one arm in a fold as the other dangled. The collars were white, and the French cuffs, where, already, links of silver—with tiny red stones for eyes of fish or butterflies—or gold spirals stuck and shone on the stiff whiteness—*alabaster, marble, sand of the Boudini's,* or *clouds.*

And when they moved, *he* packed what was pretty, writing on each box such things as "Cloth, twelve napkins," or "Lalique glasses," or "Vase, brown and gold, fragile." As Annie helped carry the boxes to the trailer, he would turn to Curtis, straddling his Schwinn, watching, and he would make a sign with his right hand, the thumb and third finger forming an "O", shake the hand. Or point to Annie and wink, say, "My little cosmopolite," by which Annie thought they were headed for a city. It was the last move.

If, in the new house, Pauline and Annie awoke at once, listening and feeling themselves as tall beneath the covers or the blankets as a hot weight as sleet or rain pebbled the windows in the climate he had chosen, they did not call out to one another. And at night while Pauline sewed, Annie took little cat-naps. It was as if she was always sleepy, or always awake and needing sleep, or afraid to sleep, or wake.

Sometimes Pauline would say to Annie in the evening, "Give me your change, I've got to go call my sister," and Annie would watch her winding down to the service station and, after a time, watch a dog following her home.

The first winter he wrote to them—stationery from The Pickwick Hotel on 49th Street, its facade etched on the left-hand corner above the address—saying, ". . . so I told Jay, sure, I'd do it for him, if he got me the residuals." Or, "If you can imagine" (Pauline would look up, say, "I can't."), "he wanted a weather show without a talent fee. So I said not on your life, baby."

Pauline would look up, say, "How he talks," and look past Annie, out the window where the clotheslines wavered, white and fat with frost.

When he sent the suit, made, it said, by Evan Picone, with pale blue and grey woven into herringbone, heavy on the tissue paper, Pauline's voice rose, wild and high: "Where am I supposed to *wear* it?" She went to stand before the mirror, turning, slowly at the onset, until her plaid dress swirled.

Walking together now to the same school, always the dog— black, with knotted fur—was behind them. All day he sat on the steps near Pauline's door. But still she wouldn't feed him, "Not *me*."

Annie wouldn't write to him. To write would be a transgression.

In the spring, he visited once, brought a T.V. set. At night he watched, his face blue in the light. He took them one day to Rutherfordton, Pauline in her suit, and showed them film clips in a dark studio. In the demonstration film he sat in a brocade chair, his legs crossed and smoke rising from his cigarette. In the collar of the blue shirt was a stick pin; fleur-de-lis in a pattern on the tie. Behind them on a white plastic chair, he smoked and said, "Not bad at all," and, "Just a little promo." Annie turned all the way around in her seat to look at him.

Now, just before the little roof closes, the brass hinges disappearing, Pauline and Annie can be seen in a room with roses, half-moons of ochre, blue light like an aura, and the sound of even breathing, sitting forward on the blue sofa, straining, looking for him behind the girl with the long, gold hair, and the curling leaves of the potted plant on a studio table.

Then, he is there before them, seated in a similar brocade chair, smoking and uncrossing one leg. He turns as an organ plays in the background. Someone is opening a door, and outside is, apparently, the broad, clear light, and, from miles away, he smiles at them.

Allegro ma non Troppo

. . . I admire compression, lightness, agility,
all rare in this loose world.

—Elizabeth Bishop

THE BOYS IN KOREA were seeping like mist, whole battalions awash. Then the cases of Spam had to be re-routed. *No one stays put* anywhere in the whole wide world, said Estelle to herself, feeling her hips part. And now *he* was off visiting his sister, high-yellow of night coming down on Pelzer, South Carolina where he had dropped them like stuffed crabs to wait, Tina and Annie at the movies where a dwarf was said to do the introductions, as in old times. Was it *healthy.*

But Johnny, lathered in himself, was clearing up a land deal before his sister went altogether out of her mind and he couldn't charm from her sixth, "high-class property." *Timing, strategy.* So he'd flashed his bright teeth, set them out at the intersection, spun off, when, in fact, no one had seen the acre in years and it was, no doubt, filled with undergrowth winding through bed-springs. No moon, no light swinging.

It was left her to get coffee at Miseldine's and a sixth of a lemon chiffon pie. She played the juke box, a song which, if years later she thought back, should have been Tanya Tucker singing Will You Lay With Me (In a Field of Stone), rawest song Estelle knew: perfectly right.

35

She loosened her shoes, red shoes but the polish chipping on her toes. And drizzling outside—the glass chilled, vapors drew in a semi-circle. She was educated, but nobody had to know necessarily. And the girls read, simply none of it in sequence. Every time they changed schools, they got promoted—Annie said, "But I don't know a *thing!*"—almost crying, until Johnny drew her into the circle of his arms and whispered, "Don't you *worry* about it, whole world's going crazy." Faith: the extra layer of skin, gen-u-ine Florida tan.

So you lift one hand and press it lightly to a cheek, tilt the head into the palm, sigh like a girl in love.

Corielli, the dwarf, pointed his finger at Annie just before the Looney Tunes and said, "We love you, Sugar," his job, to give the girls shivers, age ten and up-on-the-precipice. Then his work was over and he could retire to Joe's, sit there, have a Milwaukee, watch from afar women like Estelle at the Miseldine counter, spinning, spinning. Only it was raining.

Annie snuggled close to Tina ("Get lost") and chewed her right thumb. I don't *like* him, she said to herself. *I do not like him even if I could beat him up*, no matter Tina had leaned over and said, "You think you've never seen something like that. Well you *have.*"

And Johnny had her sweater in the car. *He* was handsome, like a movie star, only off-screen, nobody to see him but them. (And when he did go into T.V., *she* watched; and when he tried writing plays, *she* read them, said, "Well, I don't know. Do people talk like that?" And when he finally died, she was *present*, in a *dress*, white linen collar, and she wrote to Tina, "Where were you?")

So obviously Tina had been *born* mean, grew nasty. Men left her. *Estelle* knew. And now, intermission-time, it was at Tina Estelle looked first when (cold cheeks) Annie whined, "He *scared* me," that look of Estelle's meaning What *didn't* you do? *Hug her now and then.* Estelle sighed. "Well, buy some popcorn and go back in. See it twice."

Then she wrapped Annie in her raincoat and watched Tina poking Annie to the door, Annie's sleeves dangling, the coat trailing and making the loose napkins flutter to the floor. An extra button sewn on the inside of the coat hit the wall as Annie swung out. Too quiet! So Estelle played the juke box again, before the era of Willie Nelson and Loretta Lynn and all that money, little diamonds in the hairpins.

And Johnny's heart was sick, his sister Myrtle like that, standing by the window where there was nothing to see but her own reflection—her nose like his, her hands like his, the hair which never turned grey. And no words, so he felt foolish. *Some get that way* (even if the basic stock was fine, which, later, he went to the trouble to document all the way back to the Scottish hills and valleys, and sold the little book for $6.00 each to all the American relations, barely covering expenses.) "Honey?"

It was sad. At the end of an hour when Johnny stuffed the papers back into his coat pocket, she said the one thing: "The food is *incredibly* bad." Little wasp-sting in his ear. "Move over, Estelle," he would say. "Let me light you a Camel." He drove out fast, a kind of batting-hand in the night air.

"Doesn't he come back?" Annie whispered. "Why doesn't he come back?" Tina's ear was a shell.

"My fanny hurts," she said, and swung her legs up and over the seat in front of her, Annie looking, of course.

"Momma won't like it."

"You're 'The Lady'," said Tina, a hissing in the dark. "Hadn't they told you that by now?"

And so Annie was. (Time, and the cheek-bones stood out, and beneath them formed the hollows, and the eyes narrowed as if any light were too bright, lashes a shade, and above the bridge of her nose that white and wide expanse soft as lilies.)

In the ladies' room, Estelle tried to imagine *C.L.* loving *I.P.*, *1948*, Corey's ears and Irene's stiff upper lip as he lowered himself over her, her eyes and mouth like that not because he was due back at Ft. Wayne by mid-morning but because Irene knew (cello-sound in the ribs) she'd be seeing those ears, almost flapping when he moved, for all time: love, the sinking and the rising up.

And if Irene ever saw Johnny, she would faint, then, from the floor, think of asking for his autograph.

So Estelle washed her face and put on the mauve lipstick, combed her dark hair: *beautiful*, and *if* he ever left her when it faded. . . .

(Tina would visit, she would stand with her arms crossed and look at Estelle's grey hair fluffed on the sofa cushions and at the ashtray filled with Carltons and at the pink satin slippers *someone* had given her; she would say, "I told you, I told you, I told you, a million *times*, so don't you cry." And Estelle would look up from the T.V. set, her wide eyes still the most beautiful part. "Who's crying?" Estelle would ask. "Truly: *who?*" Then Tina sitting, saying, "Jesus-Christ-God-Almighty, I *mean*." How Tina learned to talk, which, in fact, made Estelle saddest of all.)

Then Johnny, in a fit of memory—whole sequences flashing before him on the road where, ordinarily, he would be watching for white rabbits—turned off Albermarle Road and onto Cox Highway and into Coy's yard where he took time to pat the dog. Then sat and watched Coy paint his warts with iodine and said, No, he really didn't feel like coffee, "Let's, what you say, make a deal."

("Coy *Who?*" Estelle would ask. She never saw him, how he sat very still under the brass lamp hanging over the kitchen table and carefully spread his right hand on the oil cloth, and would have looked startled if someone pretty as Estelle had come in, would have strained forward. In both ears were hearing aids, cords winding around to the back where they met. Estelle would have said, "Imagine," later, had she seen him once, because—if only Tina knew—the pink slippers had come from a man very like Coy, even if the cords were gone from hearing aids in the time that passed. Oh no, not wonderfully worthy to be loved. Except: Estelle had seen him under her, beside her, around her, seen how, moving, he smiled.)

Tina slept, Annie curled her legs under herself, wrapped the raincoat close-in, and waited.

Estelle heard Loo, the waitress, say, "You really ought to eat something substantial before you drown." And then Johnny was bursting in, the little bells from India jingling even after he closed the door and slid by her. "Hi, Sweets," he said, rubbed her left knee. "I got an idea."

"What about the property?"

"That?" said Johnny. "Nah." He waved a hand. "But wait here." Then the sound of bells, twice, and Johnny was propping by her stool the long box; smiling, "That."

"What *is* it?" asked Loo, walking around the counter to in-spect since, all evening, she'd felt sorry for Estelle, shivering.

So Johnny asked if they had a window (didn't notice!) and, *If* he could be permitted "to demonstrate."

"Watch this," he said to Estelle.

"I'm watching."

Loo's husband came out from the back and helped. They shoved the plaid curtain aside, got a screwdriver, and put up the vertical blinds. One side of each blind was white, Estelle noticed, and the other side was black. "Night," Johnny explained, "you turn them this way—"; they flipped. "Day, well of course you do the opposite. Classy, huh?" he asked all around, when what Estelle wanted to know was did the people inside the restaurant get the black side when it was night or those on the outside, and how Johnny had decided which. "California," he said. "They know what's what out there."

Then Loo's husband flashed them back and forth once. "How much?"

Johnny winked at Estelle. "Oh," he said, "about $19.95, minus, let's see, ten percent, since you been so nice to her"— waved a hand over to Estelle. She smiled, shyly.

Johnny counted his money while Loo went to flash the blind two or three times. "You got it," he said to Loo when he held Estelle's arm and escorted her out of Miseldine's. "You don't stay," he said to Estelle, "after you make the sale."

Watching from Joe's, Corielli leaned closer to the window and looked twice: first white, then black, black, then white. He reached for his cap, put it down, looked again. But by then Loo was back behind the counter, no light at all but from the door. Corielli mused, said to himself he thought for a minute he'd been *called*.

Estelle pulled Johnny's arm across her shoulders. He wrapped his coat around her. "See over there, Little One? We're going over and spend the whole night. Let the trailer sit, I'm in no mood to hitch it up, I got *ideas*."

Estelle laughed. "What about the girls?"

"Later," said Johnny, and paid the $9.50 at the Blue Squire, took Estelle in, and laid her down.

Undressed and, under the covers, warm. Then, suddenly, she sat up, pulling Johnny with her. "Look," she said—in the mirror how beautiful they were, the two sloping shapes of their left and right shoulders, their heads, leaning, Johnny's eyes not laughing but still for that minute—light on his left cheek and, when she raised herself, on her belly. He smiled, pulled her down, and was gentle, until he forgot.

Then Estelle slept while Johnny, stepping softly over her red shoes, went to get the girls. Estelle dreamed. (In the dream was a school friend she hadn't seen in years. They decided to go out for lunch, as in old times. "Car's broken," explained Estelle. And Louise laughed, hopped on the back of Estelle's bike and held on. "How're the girls?" she asked. Estelle turned her head and said, "Fine, they're fine. And Noah?" Louise jumped off at the restaurant and helped prop the bike against the brick wall. "Oh, he's all right." Then she touched the sign by the door, running her fingers over the raised lettering. "If he don't die." Estelle took her by the hand and pulled her to the door. "Yes, well . . . ," she said, and they looked at each other. At the door Estelle turned. "Oh mercy, somebody'll steal the bike and *then* what'll we do?" So she lifted the handlebars in one swift motion, tucked them under an arm, they both laughed, wiped their eyes, and couldn't stop laughing.)

As Johnny brought in Tina and Annie, Estelle woke, thinking: A mess is how it *is*, pulling the girls close to her. Tina said, "Jesus!" and, when they were asleep, Estelle told Johnny about Louise. "I'd *forgotten* her." Then he moved in beside Estelle, and they all slept. Sometime in the middle of the night, Tina crawled out and put a blanket on the floor.

In the morning, Johnny hitched up the trailer and put the boxes of vertical blinds there. Annie had the map and she was looking at California. "Why don't we go *north?*"

"Are you kidding?" said Johnny, putting on his nubby driving hat. Estelle held the box of Krispy Kremes on her lap. "They eat you alive up there. We are headed *West*, and"—he touched Estelle's nose—"every little town between here and there is going to have in it some Velco Blinds. Pass me a doughnut."

In the back seat, Tina had out her yellow pad and the big pencil and, after they passed the "Unincorporated" sign, she showed Annie: in fancy script, the words "crap, crap, crap" all over the page. Annie turned away, looked for cows.

Corielli got up early, his legs sore, and looked down from his room over Joe's and thought Miseldine's hadn't opened for the day. It was mid-morning before he got coffee and, because it was Saturday, missed the morning matinee.

As they drove, Estelle looked back now and then at Annie. She will iron her *slips*, Estelle thought, and it will take years before she unbraids her hair. And: *How he holds me* and *Here we are, safe and sound.* She licked the sugar off her fingers. *One day Tina in all her foolishness won't speak to Johnny at all.* What did happen to Louise?

"*Hey,*" said Johnny. "Why's it so quiet in here? Sing us a song, Annie," and he reached back to pat her legs while Tina scooted far away.

So Annie, Estelle's true girl, sang and sang, Shall We Gather at the River, where she saw, in her mind's eye, Corielli walking in naked to get baptized. And when he almost drowned, he looked up, frantic.

Sorrow

The partner is oneself.

WHEN SHE HEARD of his death, Lucy sat, stunned, saying, as if she were trying to invent an appropriate gift: *For Charlie*, who never got to see what became of her although through the years he had seen her mother, sidling, Lucy thought, up to the color red (even the hose) as her hair and skin bleached, which color she thought of as high contrast when Lucy believed it was a sign, or flag: apprehension of death happening *before* the recital, time of coming-into-her-own, fantasia of a wise man in the house and money enough to make the wisdom hold. Lucy had wanted Charlie to see her at least once more—the daughter not even close to wearing pink. Stunned, too, by what bitterness, from what old quarrels, attached itself to news of death. It was almost winter. Winter itself was dangerous.

And, if the conception of death had rubbed off on her, it was to Lucy as a locket she wore between her breasts. Men opening the silk blouse would touch the bluish hollow of her breast-bone and, not knowing what lay there, say, "Pretty," passing it by. As she intended. Such calculation in hiding what she knew, it was snobbery. Charlie would have knocked it out of her. She imagined the pure moment when no one speaks and, there, like white roses nesting in a vase, an image comes to assault the eyes, after which: no sense pretending. And, in that case, why not just laugh?

43

So, he and Lucy would have had a high time of it and, if love maintains itself at all, he would have known it then and, even later, clutching his chest when the heart went, of its own rampage, flooding the brain with colorless fluid, such laughing would have washed away, she thought, sadness: relatives hanging on to the word *good* when Lucy knew he had wanted to last, of course, forever. *Recompense, nothing!* he and she would have said in laughing.

But, as it was, he simply died, nothing sensual about it, followed by the post-ignominy of the newspapers' summing up.

The clippings fell folded from her mother's livid green note paper onto her lap, the note itself blossoming with detail all of which stank, given fact, so she refused to write her own version of flowers, and then she began to rage.

Nothing on which to fasten it, she picked up household objects and put them down again. A near-stranger wrote to her an enticing letter, which she answered in her own voice so flat with truth it was desire. To use up energy. And if he'd flown to get her, she would have gone, for the same reason: expiation, spending, two colorists' bodies mingling. Then it is as grey as dawn, they say nothing, but touch each other's ribs and the skin where the bones end—silent, pale, secret flowering.

What struck her was that, in the nearness of winter, as if she too were in a waiting-state, she began to read Proust, long after the man who had given it to her was gone, shrouded in old pain and a new life so orderly it wasn't real. And, even though, on some days, she wanted to write to him that one ought not assume the posture of nurse for one's own body when it is another's hand, cool and lifted from nowhere and unearned, that cures, she did not presume, *Swann's Way* a hand, cool as moonlight.

Lucy liked watching her son's small face mornings, when it was half in sleep, not yet tuned up. She thought: from high up, we would not appear intimate—her secret and her arrogance in one, that, for instance, her boy would enter America in this day and time with no gesture imprinted on him having come from television. So every movement was dancing. She imagined they did the old-fashioned kind remembered by others in May.

The man she saw often said, "I can like us being in the same room with the same light," and then, trying to feel less austere, Lucy began to think of light, remember occasions imbued with light.

First she remembered her parents standing on a Chicago street arguing in front of a parking meter. What in memory might have been an embarrassment—since she had been young, conscious of class differences and that they were going at it like beasts, people turning to watch—was not. She remembered the cold of the day and, above their dark coats, their faces white, the ungloved hands, white, eyes white inside of which the pupils burned black. And, behind them, the building of palest yellow brick, underneath their feet the cement sidewalk. A tableau of: when they were together. It was only after such seeming coldness and such seeming hatred, that, separate, her mother began wearing magenta and her father could say such things as, "Well, shit, I mean it gets depressing—sweating for an hour over a sweet, hot body and nothing happens."

And the time when she was newly married, living for the first season in a country of snow, and her husband decided, for amusement, to frighten her by pretending on a long drive, when she barely knew him, to be someone else—Lear, Mephistopheles, The Invisible Man, her own spectres at that time nameless. She remembered running from the car when it stopped for a light, out into silence, the snow, screaming and her breath hanging in the cold air. They were never closer because what it meant to be wed was: you hushed, and got in again, and tried to figure out *who* it was you had married, both inventing. In the snow, everything that was not snow was black.

In mourning, Lucy made this list, of light: the small white at the ends of prickly pears, damask napkins even when the meal is boring, flowers of dogwoods, omitting the stain, salt, the heads of white cats, Easter gloves, and how it was bright in the park on the day Paul said, "Don't talk—I want to show you," and he undressed, turned, dressed again.

Dear God, she said to herself because it seemed she felt so little, *do not let me be such a quick study.* Young and so full of the body's vagrancy, who would believe, if she thought such things, she could come near to bursting with laughter.

Peter knew—a teacher in the past from whom she had learned so much she wanted always to sit at his feet. So she wrote to him over distance and their encumbered lives that she needed him, and he did not reply, which she bore with the formality of one stunned, knowing with her mind if not her body that he couldn't possibly realize it was his voice laughing she wanted, to release her own.

When she went out, it was as a somnambulist, doing her work well because it was possible and therefore easy, knowing as she behaved normally that all movement in the external world could be pastiche, for she thought over and over, *When my mother dies, it will be a mess, we might not recover, and do the meek truly inherit the earth?*

It snowed; they all began to plan Christmas; it seemed she might be purified, saying of Charlie, *For heaven's sakes, he was 70 and his life was full.*

Ruse.

For Lucy also remembered, of light, the day her family was traveling by car and lost her sister. Both parents driving separate cars thought she was in the other's back seat, asleep after a rest stop. Then, on discovery and the hundred-mile return drive, they found her happily eating peach pie à la mode in the restaurant, talking with the owner, her blonde curls aglow. And it was clear she could easily have made another life, such repose in her right hand it made anguish ridiculous. *What kind of love is that?*

Lucy moved from images of white to ones off-color and soft as muted candles on a table between a man and a woman meeting for the first time. Sackcloth of the imminent infidel.

All she remembered clearly of Charlie was this joke: she, age twelve, would come in from the barn wearing his hat. He, because he had been working, would slouch in the nubby maroon chair and wait. She would go to the window, composing a face. Take the hat off, cradle it before her stomach until it would seem to weigh down her hands. From outside would come the sound of cow bells hitting against the thick neck fur as the cows loped from the barn to the pasture after milking. It would be twilight. His eyes would be on her and, when she turned, they would turn skeptical. "Well, whatcha got?" he would ask. "Tomatoes!" she would yell, tilting the weighted hat so he could see. And then they would both double with laughter while he sputtered the word, *"Tomatoes!"*

Why had it been funny?

Coming home from the Korean War, Charlie's son would not talk, but lay on the double bed looking at the ceiling, where Lucy also looked, lying beside him in her aqua pants. She felt Charlie had purposefully given her away: sparrow, little sparrow.

In the stores, shopping for gifts, it occurred to her that it was in the bountifulness of objects, ugly or beautiful, that sometimes one could summons whole the image of a person, ugly or beautiful, one loved. So she shopped as if her life depended on it, saying to herself, *mourning is appropriation*, and would have lain beside Charlie's son again.

Over and over, nettled as by misapprehension, she thought of her friend Harry as he had been in the hospital two days before he died, at 33. And she had not been prepared for the sight of him, having held back from going to his room because she was not related and felt the vagueness of what tied them together.

"You're very pretty, you know," he had said to her. But even by then what had happened had happened, though he talked and talked—lying! That fact she could not get over, when his body was nothing, the sheet almost flat and his head huge on the pillow, as he lied, because she was so young and he knew how much she needed hope, saying he would be well: the miracle of doctors and so much intelligence at work on his problem that it made you feel you knew nothing, so of course he would get up soon, and learn more. "You needn't have worn your pigtails for me, you know. The doctors said. . . ."

Lucy remembered her doubling over when she left him, holding to the white walls, because, as she saw when she entered his room, there was on the sheet over his stomach the smallest scarlet stain, spreading as he talked, and she had drawn her legs together in that instant, her body quaking, as if what was most sensual had broken through to her.

But she was not sure.

And now, she, her boy, and Paul were driving home for Christmas, so that she might see again the mother's small house and the one her father had built for himself, as if she did not bring them in her mind under one roof, her body straining forward because she felt its duration—she almost said aloud, *I'm ashamed,* as they talked of the ideal Christmas dinner, and she *would* end what she called the mourning stage.

Their car slowed and then passed a wreck. She pulled her sweater tighter, which made her turn, and she saw the ambulance moving away and, in the snow, saw left: the single patch of scarlet, when, she understood now, the afferent nerves surrender.

For, in her mind's eye, she saw herself meeting the near-stranger in a room of white, and after the laughing was over, herself resting on the white coverlet, covered in the thin white robe, absolved by sudden terror, asking him as he sat beside her, "What if we got *tired?*"

And the man beside her reached for what he had been all the time hiding, brought from beneath the bed with a smile of sadness, such as she remembered, twelve carnations of red which he carefully placed on her belly.

Lucy offered then a hatful of plump tomatoes, to Charlie, as he lay resting in his box.

Indigo

So: autumn was coming on, though you could feel it only in the morning air, the August stubble burled, and *his* beer cans exposed, like that, the blue miniature bulls glissading over the silver cans. Then, rubbing a hand over her hair, she could envision the next scene, when Rosette—what they were calling her now; they called her anything they wanted—came visiting and Ralph would be, always, on his way out to bowl with the boys. He would be in his maroon jacket; Rosette, one hand in the tiny white apron pocket, would feel that hand curl against the cloth, as if the hand could sigh. Helen would pick her up and set her on one knee. They would sit like that.

> *Sing the beasts of burden,*
> *Sing the jument in the field. . . .*

And, there, above the mantle, the portrait of the Infanta Maria-Therese, bedecked in watches. And she would never grow, her head growing heavy under the hair; the hand tiny, until, as she was, they sent her off, the red bows *enticing:* Helen *said.*

Rosette's little legs, lodged against Helen's, slept, and little prickles curled her toes when she stood. Helen tried to lift her, one hand under each arm as if they were wings, saying (Helen's hair falling over her eyes), "Well you're too big for that!" though she put Rosette in the three-quarter bed and tucked the lace-edged sheets under her chin.

49

"I'm *hot*," said Rosette, "I'm so hot," her voice trailing off. Helen was in the hall where it was dark, a cool light at its end.

"That's the shakes!" Ralph sometimes said, and when he said it, you could almost forget he ran the mill, five hundred people under him; and when he said it, his head lifted up, the blond curls shook, and you didn't remember either the pot belly, just as he didn't remember Rosette was there, sleeping.

Mornings, in his dark suit, he did as Helen told him and lifted her out, placing her feet on the black shoes where tiny tufts of cotton stuck to the soles, and he danced her down the hall, a capriole—he wouldn't have known it. Rosette's breasts, so barely there, pressed to the white cotton nightdress where, Helen said, she was going to embroider some roses, by and by. Times, Rosette fell asleep again over the cereal bowl. And then it was as if Helen herself forgot she was present, Ralph gone, loping across the field, the screen settling into the doorframe, then the flies lighting again on the mesh. Helen sat, humming, Rosette—the baby!—snoring lightly, and, outside, the autumn air.

Truly it wasn't necessary (Helen would say this herself) to ask how she got exactly where she was, crowded in the back seat of the Nash, Pauline driving, Lois by her; in the back behind Lois (the map-reader), Claire, and, in the middle of the back ("Too hot!"), Rosette, turned over to *them* now. Helen took her hand, the nails, she saw, half-moons, white as camellias.

"Blow her nose for her, for Pete's sakes," said Pauline, and Rosette sat still for it, pressing her head against the back of the seat, the eyes shut as if that, too, gave leverage. The lashes curled, dark as the hair—how unusual, in such a family, Helen herself with blond freckles, to turn such coloring excessive.

With the hanky wadded in her hands, the hands stuffed between her knees, Helen had time as they swayed over the last stretch of mountain roads (according to Lois, when no one knew for sure)—

time to see how very far Rosette's thin legs stretched, the patent-leather Mary Jane's dangling on either side of the hump of the floor. No one realized Rosette was almost grown: they said Claire (*her* name always the one striking sound) was "The Lady"—as if that meant *mean,* Claire mean as shit, which was why Helen pressed herself against the door, a balance. Yet you could feel Rosette sweating, an aura around her. Helen ballooned the sleeves of her eyelet dress—this time of calculation even Rosette wouldn't erase when she said, later, as all of them got out, "Momma thinks I'm a *baby.*" Rosette sashayed off, no one to watch her go but Helen.

Pauline was directing, the wine-red book containing all of the family history tucked under the left arm. She had a piece of paper in one hand and, according to her, all they had to do was *prove* Lucas R. Kuykendall was one of *them* (which Pauline already knew—she said she remembered holes cut out of his shoes for his bunions) and the estate would be theirs: "*Imagine* all that money. Now fan out." Helen thought that, from high up, they would look like ants crawling over the gravestones. It made her *sick.*

Months later, remembering over the supper table the expedition, Ralph would talk of the futility of "*tertiary* claims," in the way he had of putting things, "but if *you*" (he pointed the butter knife at her) "had a husband like Pauline, well, it makes it all the more understandable, when, in fact, what she ought to do. . . ." His voice buzzing, when Helen *couldn't* listen, it being, wasn't it?, quite beside the point—"ought"—in a *child's* experience of time. It made her want to hug *all* the children.

Then: the truth was she was growing old in Ralph's good providence, as if having enough of worldly possessions was in itself a season you weathered, as if such receiving made the clocks in each room as little guests who drew their own shades and laced their covers up. So, since Pauline would tell anything on herself—a lushness of indiscretion—sometimes Helen went with her driving, just the two of them. "Birds of a feather," Pauline would say, when the car in reality held even the scent of Rosette, and Claire, and Lois's hiking boots in the trunk. And Helen didn't know if she *liked* Pauline at all. It was to listen, all the miniscule pictures of listening. *She* wasn't growing fat; "*I need a man,* you know?" Pauline would ask her.

Later, in her house, as if arranging a set of slides to show in sequence, Helen would think, would say to herself: apparently *that* came either before or in-between *this,* and would envision, maybe over washing dishes, Rosette and Claire going into the restaurant. Rosette behind, Claire looking back now and then—"Idiot!"— and stopping to pull Rosette's dress over the fringe of slip showing, Rosette saying, "Well I can't help it," which Helen knew was true because Rosette *danced.*

Then:

"Two of your roast beef plates and peach shortcake for desert, *one* milk. Got it?" Claire too old to argue with, but Rosette would argue: the hand on which she wore the initial ring—"L"—twirling the fork around and around in the gravy.

Maybe the cook would come over from the grill and look at her and, if he looked down, see her stomach was still a child's stomach, that anything put in it would show. "*She's* not hungry," he would point out to Claire.

"We don't *eat* because we're hungry." Roll her eyes. And Rosette would look up at Claire: "Un-uh, Claire. *Don't.*"

"It's them," Claire would say. "Up there," and lift her fork toward the second or third floor of the hotel. "If you want to know, we already ate your Special of the Day. We ate it as soon as you opened this morning, only you weren't here."

"Claire!" Rosette would whisper. "Don't *tell,*" her lips little pouches.

But Claire *would* tell (in *some* cases: like-mother-like-daughter)—Pauline meeting Jim exactly halfway from where he was *going* to where she *would* be. "To make *love,*" Claire would say, drawing out the word. "So we have to come here and *eat* while they *do* it, got it?" until Rosette would be crying, the cook *almost* patting her dark head, Claire saying, "*Baby.*"

"Well we could leave them with you," Pauline said to Helen, "but he says travel is broadening and, besides, you want only Rosette most of the time, which, given she's smaller, I can see, but, anyway, they like it."

Helen would never tell Ralph; it might *not* be true, after all. Except why does Rosette *move* that way? Helen lifting one arm from the dishwater and looking at the inner part of the elbow, a place no one had ever kissed.

Who would love Rosette? Helen sat at the piano, making up songs as she went, occupied for months this way.

Lois, instead, took Rosette at the end of a summer; Helen said to Pauline, "A sixth cousin *removed,* and you let her go *off* like that?" But what was "off" to Pauline, now that Jim was permanently unable to fulfill his familial obligations, "as he put it," said Pauline. "Can you *get* a man like that?"

At the piano, which sat before the windows, the curtains lifting, Helen lifted her hands as if knowledge were air itself and saw suddenly that Lois would show Rosette her books, that Rosette would, later, lean over the car seat and ask Pauline, "Who *is* that a picture of over Helen's mantle?", Helen seeing Rosette's head stopped over the page showing the Infanta Maria-Therese, then the head lifting, one hand lifting, the eyes looking off. . . . In the car, Pauline would half-turn and look at Rosette, sigh. "Helen's sometimes—" and turn to the road again, the right hand free of the wheel, tapping with one finger her right temple. Rosette's eyes would broaden.

And that would be why, later, Rosette (they called her "Loo" now—what would they *think* of?) edged away at the reunion, looked down and said, "Fine."

Claire was married and gone, which made everything easier since Pauline, beginning to feel free, drifted off to help them cut the cakes, making way for Helen to slide onto the bench by Rosette and ask, "We still friends?" and tell her, Rosette's hand in hers— old times— "Don't tell your mother—it's the *one* thing that would make her cry—but *somebody* ought to mention it, so *I* will since you'll be leaving home soon—I take it on myself—you had a brother once, like you, just like you, for two days, is all, but they *act* as if no one remembers, but *I* do, and he was just like you."

"Oh, I *knew*," said Rosette, "I knew," at which time, Helen, lifting her hand, let Rosette go, Rosette whispering as Helen moved away, "And I *think* I know why *you* told me, I do," nodding.

Ralph asked, some Sundays during the summers, "So what's Loo up to these days?" as if Helen knew in certainty, when Pauline had gotten huffy talking of her. "I think she visits Jim and his girlfriend now and then, I think that's what she does." Seeing Rosette edging under Jim's arm as if it were feathered, Claire riding with Pauline in the car, saying, "The Idiot!" because: Rosette had *always* had company, her body adjusted to it, the wildness, the fear, and the silent generosity.

Would that Helen not worry: is Rosette *loved?*
Because, just as she is, in a room that is lighted with the afternoon sun edging two sets of curtains, Rosette takes off her gown and settles, waiting with one hand on the pillow, another on her forehead; *listening.*

They would be on the lawn, Ralph's cigar wedged in the mouth of a chrome penguin on the ashtray, and Helen sitting still. They would hear the mill whistle; Ralph would say, winking, "Another day, another dollar."

"I saw Rosette today."

It would be almost autumn and, in the evenings, the air would be cold, but soft as from the sea.

"She looks so calm."

Rosette would be watching him undress; *he* would be listening, hearing in how her hand moved across her forehead that she was shy, like himself. As it *should* be, Rosette would be thinking.

"And that," Helen would tell Ralph, "makes all the difference in the world."

The Formal Voice

IT IS THE WHITE MONTH NOW, when the grasses have burned and their frayed ends lie down under the dogs' feet, until the field is thatched. When a shower comes, from underneath, a steam rises. Annie imagines the field rising, shaking herself; and then you would find exposed whole families of little green snakes, curled in sleep. Beneath the straw roof, it is twilight.

Who *owns* the grey and white-spotted dogs, and when last did a flock of birds take up against the suffocating sky? She thinks: I should ride down Sugar Creek Road, honk my horn, go casually in, bringing my father, for instance, a frosted carrot cake, ask, "Do you realize this whole family has fallen into disarray?"

Her left hand, she imagines, extended to begin counting how miasma shows (the slightest sign: if this were music among musicians, atonal)—five of them. Excluding, she would say, "our children"—who are so lovely, even her half-sister he isn't sure is his child, lodged somewhere up-state. So pretty. When he leaves his billfold on the coffee table, she looks. On the back of her picture, he has written her Christian name, Tina.

Really, they should know everything about her. As it is, Annie might one day be walking with William through a K-Mart long after Sugar Creek Road has been paved and all the land beyond flooded for a recreational lake. They might be looking at electric mixers, and this girl, turned into a woman and looking so like Annie-of-the-darkest-hair, could pass by, by William's arm as she

57

spins the beaters. He could see her, the eyes, the Roman nose. A little shiver might run over him, and he wouldn't conceive why. That night, beside Annie, that delicious chill might still be there. He might turn with it to a dream-state, reach out, touch that face, as if she wanted him. Any of that might happen.

How, Annie has always wondered, have we managed so many pairs of the bluest eyes, passed on? Her father would wink, say, "Well naturally, Hon, what else?", his voice a strut, even as the August clouds are gathering.

In a week an hour's white-wash will eat into the hill on which his home-made house stands: the gullies will run red with dirt, the roads will dry red. He will laugh, say, "Had to call my congressman on that one. He said *ordinarily* they don't seed but the main-road banks. I said, 'So be *extra*-ordinary.'"

Then, in boots, walk his property where, at the perfect site, Annie will say, "I don't guess I'd put up a trailer park, if it was mine." And calling as she drives off—a lope—"Don't let the pie spoil." He will wave and wave.

Wrapping a wet towel across her bared shoulders, she sits on the top step—William's house. In the earlier days, when Annie's boy was so young he can but vaguely remember William, she would have heard his truck, its tail-gate banging. Now he slinks, the Chevy Impala quiet as a kite's tail in a sky. Though he isn't home, is only coming, has stopped at Brycey's for a Coke, she reaches out, asks, Really, My Love, what is the use? I am an ordinary woman, *esperanto,* breathing in and breathing out. Your house *is* in the country, but not so far out you didn't need a chain link fence.

His car is the color of church wine and, from it, are still falling droplets of water. He has not been drinking Coke, he has run through the five-minute car wash.

Before the heat began, she wrote often to her son, off at school, though he is young, because in the black of his eyes intelligence bloomed, opened orchids. She would write, Dear Paul, It is all going pretty much as I suspected it would, this exile, I would call it, and, still, I don't know what to do. Was it Turgenev who said, "An honourable man will end by not knowing where to live"? But never mind the pretension (yes?)—you study and play hard, I am fine.

That evening they eat corn bread, yellow squash, sliced tomatoes, and hamburger patties, a tall glass each of sweet milk, and, afterwards, on the steps, the sweet iced tea William likes. You can stay if you want, he says.

Night comes on at 8:30; all around, the houses waken to a blue light, his house too. *After we make love, the best time comes. I sit on the sofa, legs pulled to my chin, and I rock, looking out. The tips of the pines sway, encasing the least light. He sleeps, everything falls away, except that which one has imagined for a long time cleaves like skin.*

At the shop where Annie and the older sister buy dresses, the single dressing room is lined with mirrors; the women undress together. Annie doesn't buy, and when they eat at Shoney's—fried fish and cole slaw—she wants to tell Sukie the room was like a Belsen bath house, so many naked legs—fatted or already bony— veined or smooth, and ribs, and feet at once, nothing missing but the screaming and the screaming babies and the bars of soap held close as babies.

But Sukie is talking about a man she knows, who will take her to Savannah in the Trevia knit dress of blue, to dance. "You should have got yourself something snappy," she says, and Annie lets her talk, she eats. Women weren't meant to undress together. If Annie were to mention the vision, Sukie would say, straight from a documentary on T.V., "Why must you always and endlessly bring up the central image of our time?"

In cold climates, everything is easier, the body asleep in layers of shivering, and toes, encased, don't splay. When Annie walks with William on his day off, he hums, and the air is thick with the smell of barbecue.

At the reunion, Annie's mother's side, they tell her she is back in God's country, and William hides behind what they think of beards; he leans against a tree, he waits. "Resting," Annie explains. "I'm really resting." Watching her mother and Norman, whom Pauline would *never* marry, move like tandem ants from table to table, dressed alike in leisure outfits Pauline has made herself, red and red flowers.

The younger sister says to Annie, "I just bought—guess what—an Audi." But her husband runs to fat. William, Annie thinks, is the most innocent man I know. *And if ever—it will never happen—Sukie and Louise and Pauline ask, "By the way, where is your/our father living?", I won't tell.* "The meanest thing I know," Annie says to William as they drive down the mountain, "is I want her violin. It's in a trunk. She would cry, remembering." Then Annie's head dips back. Resting.

When the thunderstorms began, they went out walking less. One evening Annie finds William with his drafting paper and blue pencils at the kitchen table. Above his head shines the hanging lamp, and on his nose when the head lifts. "You see," he says, turning the paper, "we could put jalousied windows around the porch. And, under the windows, here"—he points with the ruler—"I could build shelves for your books. You could have them out—a big lounge chair in the corner, there. If you want." And Annie touches the spot on his head where, one day, the hair will fall away, where, now, the light leafs through.

In the chilly months, it had seemed less ridiculous to allow the boy to write, the one student she would ever have allowed the little notes on the thick, yellow paper, asking, "Are you coming back?" And now that it was summer, she thought often of how close to the El he lived, thought of the noise as she remembered it from hearing him talk. And she laughed too, which, if he knew, would make his face flame—that it was his shoes she had noticed, so substantial! Laced high with bright yellow laces, thick, and the soles thick, to carry him anywhere—Mondays and Wednesdays and Fridays, the shoes. "*Are* you coming back?" he asked now.

Then, in her office, his face. The room became small, Annie remembers. And though it is too hot, no breeze at all from the trees, she curls, remembering, to William's back, as if shivering.

How her father laughs: almost high, almost a falsetto, bird on a wing. She wants to waken William and say the boy's name, Quentin. *I will kneel one day and unlace his boots, uncover the white feet, and let them rest in my lap.*

From far away she heard the dogs racing across the fields, seeing behind her closed eyes the fur flatten as they ran, the indentation behind the ribs, then the jut of the leg-bones, where the fur was white. *Oh, though we may not want, we gather so many to us, the senses profligate.* But Annie does not shake William and turn him to her to listen; his sleep is like a baby's.

And when the rains cleared, she swept her father's yard of the red clay, cooked for him. "What is Tina like?" she asked. And listened as they ate.

For her birthday, William brought home a dog. It tumbled out as the car door opened and rolled on the stiff grass, scratching. From the steps, Annie watched, seeing mostly that his fur was grey and white-spotted; when he was grown, he would run with the others in the field. "Name him," called William, but she shook her head. She watched William build the dog a house, marveling at efficiency; then Annie painted it the brightest yellow.

"How long would it take," asked Annie, testing, "if someone wanted to play Mendelssohn's Violin Concerto? From scratch, I mean." They were around the Sunday dinner table—Annie, William, Pauline, Norman, and Norman's son, dressed in a business suit.

"Three years," said Pauline. "Half an hour a day, including Saturdays. Would you pass Ralph the butter?"

"Oh," said Annie, William's eyes on her. Then his right hand resting on her left leg as they drove home. "She used to play so beautifully. I could never do it."

"You could."

At his house, she sat on the car hood and watched him roll in the grass with the dog. "He doesn't stay home now," called William. "He just comes when he hears the car."

"Well I knew it," said Annie, "I did, indeed." Ah!—her father's word, rhythm of the word.

And she thought, roaming the aisles of the Food Town, dressed as if for another life, she knew now the look of William's previous women, who never paused, who dressed in slacks and, sometime during the day or night, rolled their hair—you could see the unbrushed and perfect crimp made by a metal roller. They painted their nails, they smiled and talked to the cashiers. They would hang their lingerie on the shower bar and listen to William talk about his day. Name the dog, remember to sugar the tea while it was hot. And they noticed her watching them over the oranges and lettuce; they frowned. But what did *they* know. Sometimes at twilight, while William watched T.V., she would lie in his room, its many windows open, and, from the bed, look out at the trees, time diffuse and her body motionless.

She began to stay in the room with him through the night, often moving to the chair and rocking in it, as if to hear his even breathing as she rocked, a metronome. "Annie," he called to her when she had thought he was sleeping, "I like it when you stay." *Sadness,* she would write to Paul, *is always a surprise.*

"We could let the dog sleep in the house," said Annie after it had rained. But William sighed—"You're funny."

Dear Quentin, she thought of writing, I know so much about you, and I have never told you anything of myself except what you could surmise, looking, but, of course, how much that is. . . . She did not write. And, already, it was the end of August.

"William," said Annie, "don't sleep right away. Listen to me. Do you know *why* I know you?"

Then they were together—her mother, her father, Sukie, Louise, Annie. "*That* far back?" said William, laughing. "Truly, I am sleepy."

But Annie recalled the house, how it was shaded with oaks and, far below the rise on which the house stood, ran the railroad tracks. "Every day, at 4:00 in the afternoon and then at 11:00, a train would come—that long sound. The house was set back from the highway, but in the later afternoon we could hear the traffic on the highway, the trucks going up to Asheville. The bus let us out there. I walked everywhere, all the time, walking.

"My mother practiced then—the Mendelssohn, Beethoven's concerto, Vivaldi, and sometimes, Sukie at the piano."

There would be the music, soft and then louder, the sound of the oaks, their leaves brushing, the wash on the line whipping, if there was wind. The days were long, the months of warm weather. And what was time, then? Every day, the same route while walking after dinner, across the highway and up the hills where the new houses sat, clean on the kept lawns. Closed and quiet, curtains drawn against the sun setting.

And although she was not allowed, Annie visited the neighbors, the woman who was sick and her husband, who cared for her; would stoop in the side porch by the woman's cot, and put in her hand the wild flowers—what did Annie know. *"Nothing,"* she said, her voice rising.

"It's all right, go to sleep;" William's hand pulling up the sheet.

On the woman's hand were all her rings, and on one fingernail, a blue spot; the whites of her eyes, yellow. "I *liked* her, and him, oh, him too. Of course she died." Annie turned. "I didn't expect it. How children are; Paul knows so much more. I took longer walks, that's all."

Every day up the same hill and past the same houses—one doesn't know he is remembering what he sees, but he is learning the smallest sound.

"Always there were cars going up and down the hills in the morning and the evening, taking the maids up and down. They wore bright blue cotton dresses, their husbands drove—cars of all colors, two-tone, rattling. I think I was very sad then; I didn't know it.

"I stood by as the cars passed, turned away, halfway in the weeds, and then I would start walking again when they passed. I would be almost to the bottom of the hill when the one car I remember most came by. As he passed me by, he would beat on the side of his car—maroon, I remember—with his left hand. That was all, the sound of his beating on the side of his car, over and over."

Annie turns to William. "Are you awake? *That* is what you did when you first saw me. You leaned your head out and, with your left hand, you beat on the side of your truck. I *noticed* you."

Then, for minutes, it is quiet in their room. William leans on one elbow, asks, "Does that mean you will leave me?"

Beside him, Annie is lying straight, remembering. He waits, he almost sleeps.

"*S-s-s-sh,*" whispers Annie. "Listen: the trees."

Timing

"SISTER," said Claire, limbs loose and the head cocked, prescient, as an opening flower, "you are a disease some people catch," and she did not look at Lucy but, instead, through the window, each mullion framing separate branches of the willow. They listened to the clock, the face of which hid a tiny drawer wherein their mother's emerald lay. "Learn something," she added, lifting the ties of her chenille robe and letting them fall once, another sound. The rooms were small; they could hear the breathing from the bedroom.

Lucy went to stand in Pauline's doorway, watching the sheet raise and lower before she looked at the incredible face.

Outside, a bird, perched on the clothesline, moved forward and backward in a small wind. Pauline had bought a cart to hold the green plastic garbage cans, and it sat beneath the line. Even though the bird sang, it did not look, outside, like April.

From beneath the bedspread, Pauline's pink satin mules stuck out. She had bunions. In all of what she had worn her shape remained visible—in the white sweater protrusions as if still stretched over breasts and ribs, belly and elbows. Lipstick on the neckband. On the black skirt thrown over a chair the waistband curled. A fine dust covered the dresser top and in the room was the smell of perfume.

"Just look at your clothes," said Claire, and Lucy touched the front of her blouse—silk, the color taupe, tiny pearl buttons. Inside the gabardine wool skirt was a lining of mauve taffeta.

65

"Tell her I said 'goodbye' and tell the kids 'hello' for me." Then Lucy was gone.

And, that evening, after Claire had left, Norman came to take Pauline out to dinner, to a place where the waitress knew them, so they entered to a fanfare of nylon uniforms rustling. Pauline was fat; she didn't like to be seen with Norman who was fat. His breathing was raspy and how he smoked seemed worse than her way. Moreover, he kept changing brands.

At home, Claire yelled at the children. It wasn't better when they went to their room to bounce off the bunk beds, neighbors then to worry about. Behind her, she left a trail of beauty aids—the hot rollers, two lipsticks, the three blouses she had tried on. "Hush," she yelled to them, squinting into the mirror, trying to apply mascara. "God," she said, in the car with the man who had finally come, "it wears me out," which she had not meant to say lest he think her life burdensome. "Let's go dance."

The babysitter, who had pimples, sat in front of the sliding door, bare feet on the glass, a sourball in each cheek. Noah and Faith hated her. "I'm waiting to see if this boy I know drives by," she said.

On Sundays, Claire played the organ in church and, always, Noah lost his shoes beforehand, and Claire, coat over one arm, keys jingling, would say, "All right then, *stay.*" So, his eyes big, he plopped on the couch and waited, then went to play with the older boys. And if Claire knew about his secret life, she waited for a visible catastrophe. In church, Faith giggled with the girls and moved so gracefully grown men wanted her, childhood, they must have thought, a veil one lifts.

Claire talked with the women in the office about men. "I'm going to lose five pounds," she told them, "by next month."

In Charlotte, the last sister, Pauline's "mistake," when, it had turned out, she was the most loved, laid out her silver for a dinner party, the casual set to go with teak plates and goblets and bamboo napkin rings, wealth around her like a pedigree, about which marriage Lucy thought you would have to spend so much time figuring how to dispose. But Claire, subscribing to magazines, said she'd know what to do with money, for instance buy Faith an eyelet dress for Easter. For vacations, and Mother's Day, this last daughter set up Pauline, herself, and the grandchildren in a resort cabin, food catered, the husband calling from town every two days to see how it was going.

What had become of Lucy's black onyx ring: it was in Pauline's attic, buried in fiberglass insulation. And the graduation watch was in a furnace duct in St. Petersburg, Florida. "We didn't have a furnace in that house," Pauline said. "All we had was a space heater. Remember, it *was* Florida."

"We did," said Lucy.

The weed field Claire had set on fire in Anderson, South Carolina looked just as it had the day she'd gone wild—invitational, perpetual. Not knowing whom to blame, because he was gone so much and could not tell Claire's fury from her intelligence, Pauline's husband had beaten Claire and Lucy both, The Most-Loved playing with dolls, absolved under the chinaberry tree. Welts a crowning, Lucy, that day, had become, by decision, austere, after which Claire began to say to her, "If I was you I would shave off my eyebrows, which are the only thing you have to recommend you."

Sometimes on Sundays, Pauline called Claire, saying, usually toward the end, she wasn't like some, who, when they were old, couldn't conceive of anything modern, "which," Claire said to Lucy by long distance, "is pretty much accurate."

And Lucy, having dreamed again of the house neither she nor Claire could quite remember—what state, what climate—would tell Claire a late-remembered detail. On the acre lot was cement, obviously from an old service station. "We used to ride our bikes around it." And Claire said they had been too old. "Well in that case," said Lucy, "it was where I kissed Joe Ricky the first time. I remember." But Claire told her to "get-off-that," in her mouth candy a man had given her.

In June, for her birthday, the youngest sister sent Lucy a replica of a gravestone rubbing, from Thailand, and it was beautiful, yet, somehow, not nearly so beautiful as all the things Lucy had given

Pauline. Pauline sent a card inside of which a girl was riding a cycle in red overalls, real material draped down for arms and legs. Lucy shivered, rubbing it.

Joe Ricky's mother had roasted pecans in the oven for them. And, once, she had taken Lucy's photograph on their front steps, the white in the picture Lucy's cotton panties showing as she sat, knees up. Pauline had said she was too young for see-thru's. The Ricky house had been nowhere near the deserted filling station, "after all," said Lucy. "Well drop it, for heaven's sakes," said Claire, who had, now, a regular man, flying in from Toronto.

"What's your favorite song in the whole wide world?" Faith asked Lucy, Lucy taking her to buy the eyelet dress.

"I don't have one, Honey."

"Well I do. It's Joe Cocker, singing Do I Still Figure in Your Life."

"You'll outgrow it one day," said Lucy. "When you turn twelve, I plan to give you Handel's Water Music."

And Faith said she would like that, voice soft, the blond head dipping down in shyness.

Lucy's men, in turn, offered her their permanent addresses, at restaurants, over coffee, and she was thinning.

Secret sojourner, she drove to her father's house, bringing Rothschild Brandy, which did not accompany the pictures of flashy girls he hung in the small bedroom but, rather, his clothes, all sense of taste centered there, as if anything apart from his body were incalculable. Yet, when he laughed, truly the gift was for that, this private love her act of interest and of will. Claire did not know, for instance, that, over meals, in the midst of sentences, he paused, lost, a thread missing and the silence awesome, as if it had been the only thread. In answer Claire would have rolled her eyes; she had been eighteen when she last saw him—refusal—and the youngest daughter younger still—mild circumstance.

On days when it rained, Lucy thought of the green hose lying permanently across the grass before Pauline's willow tree. She imagined that if she had helped, that day, to plant the tree, she might have come to feel at home there. She might have driven to

Field's to buy a rack for the hose, attached it to the garage for Pauline.

Then, toward summer's end, there was one last set of phone calls. "You want to know what she's doing now?" Claire asked. "She's taking Modern Poetry Writing at the college. You know whose fault *that* is, I guess."

"Momma?" Lucy asked. "How do you like it?" because, even now, she had the energy of a child, Vivaldi's Four Seasons her favorite music if, pressed, she had to say. Hope, the violins.

"Sheesh!" said Pauline, disgust an astringent. And Lucy said, almost whispering, "Well." Then Norman said Pauline was getting good at backgammon, the board his. And Pauline trying his cigarettes, *if* one judged by the ashtray, which Claire did, her intelligence faltering, like a man in love with novelty, all his women shocked. Pauline had, in fact, lost the taste for cigarettes.

And, in August, there was one last dinner with the good china, three plates on the drop-leaf table which wobbled, flowers from FTD sent by the youngest daughter, array of spring abnormal in the humid month. Over the frozen raspberry junket, Lucy asked, "Momma, I don't mean to pry, but I always wanted to know. . . ." And Claire kicked her; the table shook, and Pauline said she had to see about the coffee. Lucy innocent, Claire's eyes telling her innocence was not possible. Pauline said she wished Claire had brought the children, "especially Noah. He is a sweetie."

Then they were sitting as they had been, Claire in her robe, Lucy beneath the clock, on the maple piano bench, and all that was different was the absence of Pauline's breathing.

Norman came driving up in the mini-bus, saying as he walked in that it wasn't as if they hadn't known she would do it, "some time or another," that it was not as if Pauline had not *warned* them, "you know," he said (two words a whole wreath), reaching, picking up the empty medicine bottle Lucy had placed by the clock, reading the prescription and looking past them through the window, one hand on his stomach as if, already, he felt his weight loss in the weight of a modern world.

Lucy went to stand in Pauline's doorway, looking down at the face, it no longer surprising, time green, dangling, though she sat again while Claire named over and over the list of probable causes, litany of filling hours.

"You take these," Claire said from the bedroom when she had, finally, gathered in one pile all the gifts Lucy had given. In the afternoon light, nap-time light, the gifts looked ridiculous, especially the cream-colored caftan of sheerest gauze, with flowers embroidered from the neck to the hem. And the linen shoes dyed to match. Books, *her* favorite authors, clip earrings of gold, and the five-year diary.

By herself, Claire closed up the house, Norman saying he would go on and live where he had been, and the youngest daughter received the clock.

Her hands in dishwater, knives and glassware in the same soapy water, Claire talked on the wall phone, saying, "You all right?", to which Lucy nodded, Claire interrupting to say of Noah, "He is driving me crazy. And Faith thinks she's in love with her history teacher. He got married last week and she's acting like her heart's broken. Whatdaya *do?*" Which overflowing in distraction Claire already knew.

So, tired, in autumn, Lucy wrote the one deliberate letter Claire would have approved, and, offering herself, though Claire would have laughed at the word "offering," said to the one man she loved that she wanted to live close to him.

He might, when she was stuffy with pain, undo her, in the smallest of rooms, with, preferably, used furniture, getting her to the phrase "let's go dance," should such a gift be possible.

He might, in silence, be patient with her while she learned to await and appreciate the natural disasters, around which all the light of the world played.

Prognosis

THEY HAVE SPENT FIVE DAYS CRYING—all their bodies could tolerate. Ray had spent himself before the window of the motel room, not looking out so much as not turning around. Ann, his daughter (eleven years old and becoming already the beauty her mother had been), had stayed curled on one of the double beds, all the fingers of one hand stuck in her mouth.

Her other hand had rested between her knees—thin, scabby knees—and when Ray had turned once and noticed how her hand looked nesting in that spot, he hadn't turned again except when she said that she was hungry. Walking behind her to the door, Ray had also noticed that the tufts of the yellow bedspread had made little impressions like stars on the side she favored.

On the third day, Ann had eaten five pancakes, two with raspberry syrup, three with plain maple. After that, she had stopped sniffling, and it was then, back in the motel room, turned from her so that his breath misted the artificially-cooled window, that Ray began asking her how it had been five days before and, even, how it was now.

"Tell me something," had been the way he had put it the first time, as if the discussion of a body in repose were the same as, say, talking about the cicadas outside: fitful risings from a seven years' sloth for the purpose of breeding and dying, conglomerate sound like a moan lifting and falling on a wind.

"Anything you think of," he had assured Ann.

71

"I don't know *anything,*" Ann had answered, a temporary manner in which one might cry if the ducts themselves had dried. Her hand was damp between her knees, warm just as Ray had imagined.

They have also filled out forms at the hospital and at the Chicago office of the Hartford Insurance Company. Ray has had his personality profile determined by an MMPI test at an outpatient clinic because the circumstances of his wife's death were deemed "unusual." The results were filed, and, although Ann had said she wanted to be given a test too, the psychologist said he didn't have time to give a test just for fun.

And they have seen to the embalming. Ray had said, "The best," and Ann had asked, "What does it mean, 'the best'?"

"They look just like they did alive," the funeral director's assistant had told her.

"Not *her,*" Ann had said. "She burned. There ain't no way."

The assistant had not liked her tone.

Now Ray and Ann are on U.S. 52, driving from Chicago to Landrum, South Carolina. Ann's hair is in pigtails she has braided herself. Ray has on the pants of his second best suit, with the jacket flapping on a hanger in the back.

Since Naomi was Ray's for twelve years, he doesn't like to think of her as "it," the body, although Ann corrects him. "She" or "it", then, is on a southbound train, the travel-time to Landrum equal to that by car if Ray keeps the pace of his Chevrolet steady.

It is August, the hottest month in the latitude the two are going toward. Ray's shirt sticks to the back of the car seat and, for an instant, he remembers when car windshields cranked open to let the breeze in. Without looking over at her, he asks Ann, "Tell me how she looked when they did her up. I mean the difference it made."

"Get me a Co-cola first," Ann says, knowing he will.

After a time, Ann feels, first in her feet, the car's weight shift. They turn off, and she doesn't open her eyes; she guesses.

"Ho-Jo's O.K. by you?" Ray asks. And Ann was right.

Ray notices as he holds open her door that Ann's skin doesn't stick to the plastic seat covers. The fact gives him a chill, as if he could feel winter through his pants legs.

"She wasn't pretty," Ann says to him over the aqua and white speckled table. And, "I want a cherry-flavored Co-cola," even though she knows he isn't through with his questions.

"A little bit, I bet," says Ray when the waitress is gone.

"Not even a tiny little bit."

She watches him spread his palms, the thumbs hooking under the table edge. Then, in a single motion, he slips lower on the orange bench. He is short as it is; this way, he is her height. He won't talk much now.

In Landrum, several sisters of the Ebenezer Baptist Church are pulling ivy from the trees behind the church, intending the ivy to accent the white mums they have ordered and paid for with money from the treasury of the ladies' circle Naomi belonged to.

The gesture of the flowers is, in their minds, the least they can do, although Naomi had been for them a minor mystery, having only the one child. Too, she had spent a year at a Presbyterian College on money she'd gotten when her father died. Ray had sold his first bible to her on his way home from the central order house in Spartanburg.

The women mentioned these facts as they gathered the ivy, the unsaid "most" they could do for Naomi being, in their minds, a firm resolve to look carefully at Ray when he got back. Determine if he were the same and, if not, whether or not the condition is caused by grief or is, as they put it, "pre-fire."

Landrum is laid out on four streets, roads, really, in the pattern of a cross, the short ends being where the shop owners have their homes, the rest of the roads going for the shops themselves. Half of the cross roads run up toward Tryon, over the North Carolina state line where nobody in Landrum goes because the people there have winterized their summer houses, brought their books and pianos down from New York, and settled in. The citizens of Tryon buy whole sides of beef, building a communal locker as big as an ice skating rink on the edge of town. Sometimes farmers in Landrum go as far as the locker to sell a cow.

The other part of Landrum is filled with little houses. Down that road the spaces between the houses eventually widen. At dusk, the farmers who aren't too tired or worried sit on the side porches they have built and watch the sun go down. News goes around on these porches; if the news is bad, a person can sleep on it, tranquilized by the setting sun. And with sleep taming the body, one might not exaggerate.

"Do I look transfigured now?" Ray asks Ann.

She turns from the car window and looks at him for a long time. "No," she says.

With the news of Naomi's death, Chuck Mabry, the minister, was prudent. After Ray had cabled the news, signing the telegram "Raymond Walters, Ann Walters," Chuck had sent his wife up the road to Tryon for a *Chicago Tribune*. "Consult the text before giving out the word," he had said. The paper, almost a week old, was not in its proper order, but there, on page 53, was a picture of Ray and Ann in front of what appeared to be an office building. The headline read "DEATH RESULT OF HALLUCINATION?"

"Read it to me," Ray says to Ann when they stop for lunch, but Ann looks out the car window at the girls in their short-shorts.

Ray thinks that perhaps Ann has gotten too old to say "pretty-please" to. He edges the clipping over on the seat until the laminated plastic around it touches her leg. She jumps.

"We don't need that, I said!" She has backed up against the car door. "I *told* you. They don't know anything anyway. It was just some boy. His teeth were bad. White socks, he had on white socks, and you told me when you went selling you never wore white socks. *He's* the one who wrote it. *I* got it all up here," she says, tapping her forehead. "Every bit." And Ray lifts up the warm piece of plastic as quietly as he can and he tries to chew slowly.

"Well," he says. "Well?" He rubs the paper napkin over his knees until it looks slightly curved when he holds it up— something to do while he waits.

"They tried to clean her up. Whole parts of it is off her hands. They couldn't get her face all clean. They put rouge over it, that's what."

"Well," says Ray, starting up the car, "her hair. She had the prettiest hair."

"That's true," says Ann. "It *was*." She begins to hum, by which she means nothing, except that she is thinking.

The women who are gathering ivy behind the church are discussing the event, the more so because the facts are scanty. Ray, one of the women remembers, had said once about his door-to-door selling, "It gets so hot I look at the women and think: why, I'll just go on inside, have that glass of ice-cold tea and stay on. And what would Naomi think of *that?*"

"But we knew, too," another woman says, "if he quit it wouldn't be to farm—too handsome for that, you know." They all nod.

Apparently, as they say to one another, their eyebrows rising with the word, Ray had packed up his family as if they were going on a camping trip, taking the Coleman stove and the outdoor lantern. "His good clothes," one of the women remembers. "James saw them off and he says Ray had on his brown suit, the one he wore when his mother died."

Then, in the state park—the women had never heard of it— Naomi was cooking, and then the charcoal fire went out. "What happened to the Coleman?" a woman asks.

"Didn't say," another answers, meaning the news clipping.

Naomi called Ray over and he put kerosene on the coals. Then he went back and sat down on the bench where he had been paring his nails. Naomi put the match on the charcoal and then the kerosene exploded.

"'*Whomp,*' like Ann told them."

"Ray got transfixed," one of the women says. "I've seen his mother like that more than once. We used to admire her, and Ray got it from her, even if he wasn't immersed. In his blood. Ann told them. . . ."

"I got it right here," says Rebba, the youngest of the women *and* Ray's littlest sister. She reaches into her apron pocket and shows them the clipping from *The Tribune.*

"Where did you get *that?*"

"Sent Lewis up; he went."

"Lewis did that? Well, you get to read it, I guess."

Rebba runs a finger down the column, then looks up and recites, "'He thought it was him. He forgot it was her. He rolled his own self on the ground and he wrapped his own self in my sleeping bag. He didn't know it was her burning. He thought it was him.' Ann said that," says Rebba.

When Ray and Ann make the change-over from U.S. 52 to U.S. 25 and have to wait at a railroad crossing, Ann turns to Ray and says, "I've decided."

"What?" says Ray slowly, like a man asleep. He had been thinking that *he* has never been on a train.

"I'm joining you," says Ann, "and not getting saved."

A big, slow-moving smile spreads over Ray's face. He reaches over to pat Ann's leg. "Well," he says, his hand moving staccato on her leg, "I do like that!"

Ann is counting the cars of the train. As the caboose goes by she tells Ray, "Thirty-nine. *But*," she adds, "I am still going to Sunday School and, after that, to hear Preacher Mabry preach." She looks at Ray.

"Don't make sense to me," he says, then, in Naomi's stead, corrects himself: "doesn't."

"Learn," says Ann. She sits up and puts her hands in her lap. "I am going to learn. *Something*, that's what." And she gives Ray a smile he can't place.

Ray is thinking: Is Naomi on that particular train, yes or no?

After Ray has driven a mile or so, Ann says, "Like, you're probably thinking, 'Is *she* on that train back there.'"

"Was not."

"And what *I'd* like to learn, for one, is how many trains start out in Chicago. Then, how many make it to where they was sent."

"Trains don't have wrecks," says Ray.

"*Some*times they do," Ann says. "Remember that one went over halfway to Greer, and the grapefruit and oranges and even the U.S. mail was spread all over the road, and everybody rode by and ran over the grapefruit and oranges and. . . ."

"Hush," says Ray. "Turn on the radio and hush-up."

"We're too far out," Ann says, "and besides, nobody could get *you* to hush." She reaches up and takes the newspaper clipping from the dashboard. "Says here. . . ."

But Ray snaps the piece of plastic from her hands; he slaps her with it on the legs and then he holds it up over her head. His head moves back and forth from the road to Ann. His eyes are large and the lashes don't shut at intervals.

Ann looks at him for a long time. Then she sticks a handful of fingers in her mouth. She leans her head back on the seat and pretends to sleep, although she forgets to stop jiggling one foot that is crossed over a knee.

After a time, Ann's head slips on the seat, and Ray carefully pulls her over. Her head rests on his shoulder. She snuggles in, and Ray thinks she might be awake.

In Landrum, it is the last night of the revival which hasn't been as elaborate as in previous Augusts. Money is tight all over. The minister was afraid to commit his congregation to paying the expenses of an out-of-state revivalist and since he considers himself as good as anybody *in*-state, he has been preaching the entire week himself. The Coleman Family Quartet has come up from Charlotte free since they have relatives in Landrum.

At twilight, most of the members of the Ebenezer Baptist Church are preparing to go. They don't dress much, knowing that on the last night almost everyone will rededicate himself—not a particular and anguished surrender. This night the only person who might be saved is Jesse, the twelve-year-old son of the Bemans, and this prospect doesn't motivate them much since the question wouldn't be decided until 9:30 or 10:00.

Those who are going to church don't eat a heavy supper. They have been in town until late afternoon and so they snack on Nips crackers, some pickles, sardines, and soda pop. Jesse eats, but what he eats gets stuck in his throat.

After the singing of "Bringing in the Sheaves," Chuck Mabry tells the congregation what has happened to Naomi, announcing it in a way one might to someone hearing it for the first time, which he considers sagacious.

He retells the history of Ray's family in the church—"long but one-sided, as they say," which gets a laugh, even though it is the same thing he said when Ray's mother died. He reminds them all that Naomi attended circle meetings faithfully, which, he tells them, is all that could have been expected, "Raymond having conceded to play with the outside chance of eternal fire himself."

He lingers over his description of Ray's mother "in trance," reminding his congregation that she had tried to save all of her children. "Whupped 'em some," he says, turning to wink at Rebba at the organ.

Then, when he senses that his congregation is restless, he tells them all how he's decided to think about what has happened: with grace and good-forgiveness and a sense of predilection, "since we all are in the Lord's mercy and have no idea what might or might not be required of us. My text tonight. . . ." And he is into the sermon now. Those who will sleep through it are beginning to nod, and those who won't have fixed their eyes on him.

"He didn't say a thing about Ann," a woman whispers to her husband. "It's *her* we'll have to see to. *He* won't let us do a thing about *him*."

"Shush," her husband says. So she sits back to think.

In Knoxville, Ray takes Ann to a shopping center. He has begun to feel grubby and thinking of his own clothes has made him look down at Ann's dress. "I'm going to buy you a pretty dress to wear," he tells her when he awakens her. "Then we'll eat supper."

"Black," Ann tells the clerk inside the children's shop.

"Oh, no," says Ray. But the clerk is already explaining that they don't really carry black dresses except in winter—"Little velveteens, you know."

"I want one of them," Ann says to her. "I been thinking while I was sleeping what kind of material and I couldn't think of the name of it. That's it."

The woman looks at Ray, who doesn't look at her. "I'll go see," the woman tells Ann.

"I been wanting to ask," says Ray, "about the shoes they put on her. She shoulda been wearing shoes. I told her. It mighta helped."

"Wouldn't have helped," Ann tells him.

"Well, what kind are they now, then?"

Ann fingers the hem of a dress. "First," she says, I thought they was like mine—black ballerina. But then I touched them."

"You did?"

"And then I could see they was just paper. Nice, thick cardboard, but that's still paper. So she has got on paper shoes, with little string ties."

Ray tries to imagine them.

The clerk brings out a dress covered with plastic wrap. She pulls the covering off and turns it before Ann.

"I like it," she says. "I'm going to put it on and wear it."

While he waits, the clerk asks Ray how the weather is outside. He says that he doesn't know.

At the restaurant, Ray says to Ann, "You'll burn up in that dress."

Ann looks at him.

She eats and she is careful not to spill ketchup down the front of her dress where there are little yellow stars embroidered on the bodice, with a crescent moon over what would be her left breast if she were older.

"I'm bone-tired," Ray tells her. He hardly eats.

Over her pie, Ann says, "They won't like it. We said we was moving and now we're coming back. People don't like that, I know they don't."

"Well," says Ray, drawing out the word.

"And we'll spend the insurance money in town, unless we go up to Tryon, which we hadn't ever done before. And they won't like that. They won't say it, but they won't like it."

"Well," says Ray.

"So"—Ann licks the fork with her tongue, turning the tines around and around—"so I've decided: like in the Bible, 'Yes,' and 'No' is what's supposed to get you saved or burnt in hell-fire, so I thought while I was sleeping, I'm just going to tell them 'Yes' if it's 'Yes' and 'No' if it's 'No.' No use explaining."

When Ann asks Ray for his wallet and goes to pay the bill, Ray imagines Ann never sleeping. Or, he thinks, she will say she is going to sleep and then she won't sleep. Or she will say she is going to stay awake, and then she'll sleep. Or she won't say which, and there won't be any way to tell when she is or isn't.

"Let me sit here and finish my coffee," he says to Ann when she returns. After Ann sits, he asks her, "When she went to sleep in the car. . . ."

"It wasn't no sleep. She was unconscious by then."

"Tell me again what she said right before that. Just once."

"Promise?" Ann asks.

He nods.

"*Lie,*" Ann says.

"Well I can't help it," says Ray. "Pretty-please?"

"She said, 'Make sure he knows it was me,' is what she said." Ann picks up her Coke cup and chews on it. "Then she said, 'Make sure he knows it was me, and, if he knows that, you'll be all right.' So then we got to the hospital and they didn't want me to go and I climbed up on you, that's when I told you, like she told me to. And then we went in and she was dead, and. . . ."

"She was *sleeping.* I *talked* to her."

"She wasn't sleeping!"

"Was," says Ray. "I went over and I had you with me and we touched her arm and I told her I was sorry."

"Lie!" says Ann. "Dead. And you know it. We looked at her and we didn't turn to stone. You know it," says Ann, getting out of her chair.

"I thought. . . ."

"Say it," Ann says to Ray. "You say it. You didn't ever get to tell her you was sorry. And besides," Ann says, moving back to her chair, "she wouldn't of heard you anyway."

She picks up her fork and turns it in the leftover food. "But I wisht you'd say it. I wisht. . . ."

"I knew it," Ray says softly, and then he begins to cry.

"Won't help," says Ann. She takes him by the arm and walks him outside and tells him to wait while she goes to Rexall to buy Kleenex.

But he stops crying before she returns. Waiting and looking out at the parked cars and the white lights, he doesn't feel tired. He thinks he might not ever get tired again, unless it's out of habit.

They went through Tryon at 11:30. A number of the cafés were still open, and that surprised them. Ray drove fast between Tryon and Landrum, and Ann sang all the songs she knew because the radio station was off the air.

"Is that all you know?" Ray said. "'Abide With Me' and 'Standing on the Promises' and all them? Don't you know anything popular?"

So Ann stopped singing and then she began to call out the names of the people who owned the houses they passed.

The train carrying Naomi was on schedule. A number of the townspeople got up for it, or they had stayed up. They were tired from the long service at church. Jesse hadn't gone up front to declare himself until they had sung the chorus of 'Just As I Am' twelve times, and then they had had to get in a line to shake his hand.

They didn't talk much because they thought they ought not to. They watched Ray and Chuck Mabry officiate at the transfer of the casket from the platform to the Royal Hall Mortuary down the street. Preacher Mabry said it gave Ray something to do.

"Well, sure," said Rebba, speaking for all of them. "But what about the viewing of the body? I mean, what time and all?"

Ray kept a hand on the silver handle that was warm to his touch. He looked at Rebba as if he hadn't heard her, then he looked over at Ann. She was waiting. "Well," said Ray, "me and Ann, we thought that this time, considering—in consideration of her, we thought. . . ." Ray looked at the ladies from Naomi's circle meetings. "Ann?" he called. "Ann—she'd be the best one to tell you, I mean. . . ."

"No," said Ann.

"'No' *what?*" Ray asked her.

"No viewing of the body!"

"What?" said Rebba, edging herself toward Ann.

"*No.*"

"That does it," said Ray. "Let's move her now, careful as you go."

Some went with Ray—the men mostly—and some stayed on the platform where Ann was waiting for Ray. Everyone who was with Ray thought he should have stayed with Ann. Everyone on the platform wished he had gone with Ray.

It was a let-down.

Sounds were what Ann noticed—feet shuffling, women nudging their children for talking too loudly, and the children saying "Will you quit it, that *hurts.*"

The women were solicitous to Ann. When they asked her if she were "all right," she said, "Yes and no." It gave the ladies a chill.

Jesse went up to Ann after Ann got herself alone and he said to her in a whisper, "I wish I hadn't of been saved."

And, since then, it has all gone much as Ann had imagined it. She couldn't, however, remember where she herself had been standing when it happened, as if the eyes had detached from the body, a fact she may or may not get over.

And it took her a long time to realize that learning led from one thing to another, out of Landrum, for instance, which, of all the things that surprised Ray, surprised him most of all.

Yes, she is beautiful, as Naomi was. Looking for a long, long time, a man might think *he* could open her.

When she moves, she moves as if time were everything.

Ineffable

That I may reduce the monster to myself,
and then may be myself in the face of the monster.
                        —Wallace Stevens

I HAD NOT PLANNED on an education; I wasn't going to *become* anything, as if, for so long, that which was animal in me had not enacted its first shedding. Earlier, when I was a child and my mother said to Jim, each year, sometime in November, in some natural forest, "Don't you think they ought to be in school?" (softly, as if she had no right) and he answered (after his eyes took in the panorama), "They can *read,* can't they," I remember thinking, That's true. A surprise—my reading: habit close as breathing, intimacy of intimacies.

From real life, the eyes ached. It was the hey-day of Billy Graham. He talked about things coming to fruition—my mother said, "Hush, I want to hear." But he meant death, opening sky, and the ascent. I had such energy my body ached, inherited from my father, except Jim always knew where he was headed, his secret.

In the single beds of my childhood, my sisters and I played a game of kicking one another, which, as I look back, was painful, and, yet, we felt no physical pain. We couldn't wear ourselves out. And, had we been able, had someone been in charge, would it not have been a luxury? Our mother did not shrink in front of us, she turned her nerves inside out until it seemed everything not meant

85

to be exposed was raw. And Jim, who loved all of America he could see, kept singing.

I might say the contrast made us think. But it was our bodies lost in thought. And did I need look up from the books for that?

Then, when I was, as they say, grown (since I had had the baby and time enough to know still I was in the back seat of my father's Packard, starched in the middle, and not ready for one man's Street of Lacy Trees, though he had been gentle as such blossoming), *then* (my boy and me drifting like pollen): along came Milo. It can happen if, as I did, you peek out there now and then on the outside chance there's been a speed-up, not simply memory touched off by shadow (Jim saying beside every hot springs, "Imagine that."), which is what, I thought, objects contributed. I loved Emma Bovary as I loved myself. What *is* tragedy?

Milo was eating salad, with cut red cabbage for color. Had it been a more substantial meal—more array on the table—he would have let me pass. He was bored and he was handsome. Always, my mother had told us, girls of our breeding did not wear golden anklets in summertime, which would have been for men like Milo. I remembered, I remembered the tiny filagree, and, as for the breeding, I was teaching my boy to love the world. Jimmy saw Milo looking at my eyes, and he tugged my skirt. "Yes, yes," I said, vague to presentiment outside the family stirring in the car.

When, later, I heard of Milo's birth-place, the only home (incredible) until he left to way-lay me in the street, I thought, Had *I* been given so many rooms, I would have, ice-cold floors notwithstanding, spread my limbs across them and lifted up. I would have come, finally, to rest my wings on the window-ledge, and looked at the trees ascrape on the frosted glass.

But Milo sat before the stove, boots smoldering on the door and, in the crush of brothers nudging, watched the tiny flames visible through the cracks, and conjured up a set of eyes like mine.

Overhead, I *might* have been just lifting up, my sisters with their ballerina slippers hot on the grate. Circumstance is what those authors gave their women; *I* knew.

"*Talk* to me," said Milo. "Tell me what you *know*."

Somewhere in the middle of my Age With Milo, my father called on his way to Arizona or Portland, Maine, or, maybe, the hinder-parts of Moonville, Georgia. He wanted to hear how his daughters, as in *lay of the land,* lay, and I was the only generous one. "*So,* Sweets," he said. And, to have something to mention, I told him Milo, before making love, always read me a story, then blew the candle out. My father said, "Aw, Honey, *shit.*" I don't think he would have heard me had I told him it was a sort of trade to Milo.

"Just use the word in the way you know by feel," said Milo.

In a recent dream, I was fondled by a cat, his body elongated and the fur fluffed. But, seconds later, on the steps, he hunched his back, squaring off with a postman who had come to deliver a painting. I stood in the dream at the screen door and watched them, two duelists, over my body. The postman's back was curved, the head dipped down, hands floating at his sides. The painting, as it turned out, was inconsequential, changed by this scene of early winter. Does it matter from what world images arise?

For Milo, the backdrop I mentioned was of my mother in one of the houses we turned to in cold weather while Jim roamed. Each house was tiny, but, every Sunday, even in the sleet of February, we stretched the washed lace tablecloth on the wooden drying frame outside, signpost of an elegant life we had heard of. I told how her head looked thrown back when she had finished playing the violin—legs apart and such joy in her eyes I wanted Jascha Heifetz to come look. And, should Milo want accuracy, I told of her current enshrinement, in *one* tiny house, in *one* small place, now that Jim is over and done with in the flesh of her flesh; and she is selling real estate. In any empty foyer, her arms are weeping for her arms. She is not *listening.*

In other words, I gave Milo everything I had but the visible act of wasting. Ha! I said to myself on leaving Milo, He didn't take little Jimmy into account, how so much of me is saved for him it would astound.

So: goodnight, goodbye; I am not ashamed.

And Milo said, "You're strange. You're very odd. I don't think you realize. For instance, you hardly pay attention."

Looking down at Jimmy, I thought of Milo's gift to me. I thought it was a stage appearance he had given me, without proper notice, no advance training, no estimate of the crowd. I thought: Milo might be right. He *frightened* me (*this* is how they do it), which is how I came to know who *else* loves in books those I love, cacaphony of lovers.

It might have worked, I might have been wrested for this world, brains teasing brains in the enormous school of ivy where, but for the ridiculous outfits of the times, and phrases jangling like neck-beads or Russian crosses against tufted chests, one might have imagined he was learning the historical dance. Once, during a class held on the grass, I sang four Wycliff songs for all of them—and told Jimmy when I got home. Oh, it was possible to think I might not have embarrassed Milo in the public eye, given time. I might have wakened from my dreaming.

I think one person can be prelude for another, antithesis or accentuation. In this case, Peter did *not* talk or want to talk. He found me in all of that huge place and he said, Want to go for a walk? "Oh yes," I said; we laughed. Want to come to my house? he said, at which I laughed and then said, "Yes, yes, yes," as little Jimmy might. Only once did my voice waver, saying too much. His head bent over the buttons of my blouse, I asked, "Why *me?*", touching my collarbone. And Peter shrugged. He was himself that thin, accouterment greedy Milo would not have understood. My toes itched as if a bird's toes. If, one day in the park, in full sunlight, I had cocked my head and asked, "Do you think I'm strange?", he would have said, "Sure, why not?", the shrug *almost* perfect grace in an outside world aburst. It was almost enough.

Everything is an adventure, one way or another, you know?, I said to Jimmy. When we get through here, we'll try another place—how about that? (Yes, yes, yes!) because: of sights. When Peter and I walked, always we took the same streets, where there were trees and houses with stained glass windows, the rooms of Jimmy's friends, and cats. And, too, high up, on the top floor of Little Sisters of the Poor, home of the old, the face of a woman looking down on us.

For once, I did not nudge Peter, my seeing her and her knowing I saw her a privacy. I almost waved. But every day there issued from the gates a procession—of doctors or of mourners or of vans with flashing lights, with figures inside wrapped and all white but for the eyes, even the hands held to the collarbones white, curled, and stilling. I thought: she knows what my mother always knew.

And I saw above our car, in the desert or above a stand of pines we camped under or, simply, beside the sun as another face: her face, watching. My child's time slipped away, our car itself so small that we, inside, hidden by the roof, might have disappeared.

One afternoon, the woman was not there. As Peter lowered himself over me on the last day, I said to myself, I will miss you both.

Because he had asked, one day while visiting, "Well, what did they *teach* you," I read my father a story, an Italian story set in the mountains where no one went. I thought the absence of modern objects would help him concentrate. And he said, stopping me, "That's too *sad*. If I thought life was so sad, I couldn't go *on*."

It was the most of himself he had ever said, so long! after my mother's eyes had narrowed and it was not certain she could, again, be startled.

We might not need, always, to close the eyelids of the dead, revelation-by-chance the certain happenstance. So *who*, I want to know, would swear Emma was not *tragic*, in even, as the saying goes, the classical sense. *I* give her to my father, a present for anyone in the time of his time.

And now (*Milo,* duplicated the world over), I am in self-reserve, retiring, going toward (by stepping back, now that Jimmy is mostly grown, raised as all children should be, as an original wonder) a resting-up.

I would that I will be loved by a man who can see me perform in the very world and not overly believe a word of it, himself, for me (And oh Ariel, if I could, in your cold preserve, *tell* you) the earthly embodiment, Angel, omitting, as I would, *necessary,* since we are all, in our bodies (strummed), humble, I think.

Ligature

The world seldom changes,
but the wet foot dangles
until a bird arranges
two notes at right angles.
—Elizabeth Bishop

CARLOS WAS DYING, but what, now, of that, since he had cut her off, his body, still walking about, the shaft of the lily iron; and, especially on cold days when the winter sun shone brilliantly, she would imagine the detached, barbed head of the iron set on a damask cloth, amongst silver, stemmed crystal, gold-rimmed plates, and the scatterings of salt around each miniature swan. Light would come through the voile curtains and the dark, polished floors would shine. He would take off the pea jacket and seat himself at the head of the table in the wing-back chair; he would smell of fish.

There is a feast to which I can't get myself invited, she would want to tell Quentin—what she had named him, to be baroque, since what was he, after all, but a boy. As it was, she told him nothing, restraint emblazoned.

And acquaintances would not let her sleep a season through because, as all the world knew, Carlos had not been hers by any law except that the birds and beasts and fishes moved by. Though she did dream. He would lift the fish knife, saying, "Do you know where I learned to use this?", beginning a tale to see her through

91

the night's opacity, a tale which would have happened before her time with him—fact, not even a taunting. And she would wake so angry.

Her name was Anna-Marie, and her mother, the first Anna-Marie, had played the violin, which everyone but the daughter had forgotten, this quality, of her memory, if this were logic, adjunctive, a grass best burnt-off.

"Anna," Carlos began to call her, as if to truncate even the name although she could use logic herself and say that it was he hadn't time now, efficiency was everything . . . she was receding, if she imagined his perspective, as a girl on a beach waving the fisherman off, and he draws his attention to the height of the waves. Her ruffled apron would appear, finally, as a gull swooping low on the bar of sand.

"Drive me, this winter, to the places I have to go," she said to Quentin. "I'm distracted," and, You're so very young, she added to herself—benefaction, Carlos thinning, the crystal he lifted in the morning sun shaking so in his hand that its curves threw colors of salt against the salt.

If Carlos visited her, she would light a fire and, by it, undress him, rubbing the scars and feeling, almost, the word *futile* sewn into them. "What have I learned?" he asked sometimes. Others, "I'm learning a lot, you know?" But he would not say what he was learning. She rubbed a finger across his ribs, as if they were gills, opening and closing.

Once, her mother, visiting, said, "Listen—the Chaconne, by Vitali. I played that for my recital. I was sixteen. Can you imagine?"

So, obviously, Anna had been wrong, on the face of it, her mother remembering too. And yes, Anna could imagine it: the dark head thrown back, the fingers moving so fast in the hall's spotlight they were finlike, the long, white gown moving in ripples, and the black eyes open but seeing nothing apart from the notes on the page made apparent only by memory—from the time she had been alone, in another room, when, in the beginning, the notes would not remain singular and the fingers would not fly, when the counter-rhythm was her sighing, when the world would be hers *only if.* . . .

Now Anna watched her walk, a heavy clump, clumping, the body so weighted, *could* the arms lift and was there, still, a place next to the collar-bone where the violin could rest, and would not the chin blister, fester, become, itself, weighted. . . .

Time makes its own concoctions/ sweet or leavened with thorns. Anna would write this, remembering a particular Easter bread, herself seated at a long table and asking if she might be the one to break it open and find the single egg baked inside.

If it were gray outside, Carlos would rise from the wing-back chair and pull the velvet drapes, light the candles, sit again. He would, sometimes, look across the expanse of white to the end of the table where sat the identical chair, and raise one hand as if he were speaking, punctuating a thought with the hand. Then he would look at his hand, at the empty chair, and lift the crystal bell beside the plate, ringing, ringing. But of course no one came and, in fact, as the bell was rung, he would forget the hand's motion, its use to him connected to the bell, and put it down abruptly, annoyed at the interruption.

Across from the podium from which she would read what she had written, Quentin would sit, watching, and, from where Anna stood, light on her and on the pages, the room otherwise dark, she would see Quentin in only the vestiges of this light, as if only he and she were in the room.

"What haven't you seen?" Quentin asked her, his eyes always on the road as they drove, as if to keep a proper distance, when, Anna said to herself, he knows I am learning his body. Driving, driving all night, through rain clouds which hunkered, to the sound of wiper blades, his breathing, her breathing; and music, low and swollen, at once, as if Schumann had come to play pool and warm a booth, the same song, over and over, all of this an estuary.

"Oh," Anna would say, lifting a hand in weariness and letting it fall again into her lap, a napkin. And then, remember the first

Anna-Marie's sense of manners. So, slowly, she would begin a sort of recital: "Oh, the insides of roadside diners. . . ." He would laugh. And bars into which men wear cowboy hats while swinging the low-slung girls, eyes bright as stars. And the flat Indiana moon as the sky clears. . . . His wrist, flicking; the toss of his head. *Do not worry,* she would want to say.

As the wind blew, the snow began to pile against the house so that it appeared shrunken. At night, especially, the windows shook. Each afternoon the walks were smooth with snow where the wind had blown it to cover any footprints. When Carlos came up the drive, his would be the only marks on the snow, which imprints would disappear as they drank tea, listened to the music her mother had played. Then he would wind down the drive through new snow; he didn't notice—she would ask him, and he would look at her as if there were something *she* had forgotten.

Often, he would forget the formality of the table and rest his head on the white cloth, pushing aside the plate and the crystal, the bell, which would ring once. He would turn his head toward the window and close his eyes. It would seem that he was sleeping, and then he would rise to pull the curtains apart, sit again, and so he would fall asleep with light on his face, or seem to fall asleep, for it would be startling to watch him reach behind to pull the pea jacket down from the chair and around his shoulders. She would look for a long time, since, at any moment, the jacket might not lift and fall at the shoulder she watched, as if, her body straining forward, she was to perform the word *Now,* reach in, cover the head.

"You remember Quentin, don't you?" she would want to ask Carlos, in apprehension that he would see the two of them together and notice that they, too, were being closed off, and Carlos would look at her and ask, "So soon?"

She would be able, then, to watch his eyes narrow, and the word "Basta" spit from his mouth, and he might, then, lift her and carry her upstairs, pull the covers from the bed and place her precisely as he remembered on it, and when he would undress, he would, suddenly, be resplendent in all the lost flesh, and he would walk, naked, to slam the door, as if downstairs Quentin were listening.

He would, then, open the shades, as if to signal himself, and then he would lower himself over her and ask, "*What* did you say?" Until she would whimper and tell him that the boy had only lifted her hair and touched her, once, on the back of her neck with two fingers, which would be a lie, and Carlos would know it, and lift her head, throwing it back into the pillow, saying, "Nothing happened, *did* it," and she would smile, slowly, and pull his face to hers. "No."

On another visit, her mother said, "Do you think, now that you're grown, we can talk as equals, because there are things I want to say and, yet, feel that I can't," *her* eyes narrowing as Anna answered, "No," watching her mother's heavy breathing and the sagging of the upper arm which her mother held crossed over her head. Such meanness: Carlos *will* have company. And when Quentin called, she said, "Take me to all the places I haven't seen."

For nights she didn't dream, and what was Carlos doing then?

"Why do you do this?" she asked Quentin as he held the umbrella for her against the sleet.

She watched him think. "I don't know." And, "Come on," taking her into the bar where men wore cowboy hats as they danced and the girls' silver belts caught the light and spun it. Sometimes she would laugh, watching, and know he saw her laughing.

"I like it," she would shout over the music. "And my mother, you know, would be horrified," and laugh again, naming them, in such a place: Bach, Beethoven, Mozart, Mendelssohn, and—the fifth finger—"never, oh never, Rachmaninoff."

"*Never?*" he would call from across the table.

Getting up to sit beside him, she would shake her head, "Oh no," and let the hair fall forward, tuck her legs under her, their shoulders touching.

But, driving to her house, when there would be nothing she knew to say to him, she would think of her mother's question, say, in the formal voice of an amendment: Another time we'll talk as equals, or, at least, something will *happen* . . . you should *know* that, so much music . . . herself shivering, inadequate to this speaker's chore, and Quentin seeming older.

Then, as the rage of winter slackened and the crusted snow filled with footprints—his, hers; his/hers; light and heavy/ light and lighter—*if* Carlos were watching, if he were watching her move around the kitchen as if to a tune, if he noticed her blouses were bright colors and that she wore a belt of turquoise and silver, if she did not, over time, first remove from his soup the lemon and then the rice, if she did not watch him coil on the bed and raise his knees to his chest, skin deeper into the covers which looked like whitecaps—if she were not jealous, herself, of him—*then*. . . .

Anna would stand before the mirror, mornings, and examine her face, surprised that it was the same. I'm learning so much, she said to herself, but I don't know what I am learning. "What do you think?" she would ask Carlos, and he would shake his head.

It was warming outside, so he would take her arm, they would walk in the patio. He would sit at the wrought iron table and rest his head on the table, so she put embroidered cushions on it. From the window of the kitchen, she watched the first birds fly down to pull the colored threads from the flowers sewn on top.

You should worry, she wanted to tell Quentin as she watched him spray the patio, watched the water arc and fall, filled with colored light.

She would think Carlos watched them play under the hose, that he saw her shivering with delight.

From where he sat, he could see through the voile curtains only the trees, and, at first, he would turn his head, resting on the table, toward the trees; feel the new coldness of the cloth on his cheek, and think, because the new foliage made the room darker than on the sunny winter days, that it was still February, and he would almost sleep again.

He would slip one hand beneath his chin, raising his head, and, with the other hand, he would move aside the candle holders, touch the dried wax. He would shake his shoulders free of the coat, look up, then, and smile at Anna, or what he thought was Anna.

When he lifted his head, he could see that he was wrong; the fact made him smile, one eyebrow raised. Then he was cold again, though now he could see through the curtains that light shone through budding trees. Ice would have broken near the shoreline and the sun would come earlier. He pulled the coat close, then, and rested his head again on the table. He let his arms drop to rest on the padded chair, and it seemed he would sleep.

"Now?" Anna whispered, thinking it would be time to call Quentin for his help.

And then Carlos lifted his head. He nodded toward all the empty chairs, and shook his napkin out—a flourish—and tucked it into the collar of the checkered shirt.

If you don't mind, Carlos said, as they brought in the wine and the platter whereon lay the perfect fish. And, as Anna watched, he ate it, from the tail to the eyes, then, gently, with both hands, lifted up the perfect boat on bones.

When Quentin came, she put one hand on his cheek, by which, but for memory, she set him free.

Fable without End

IT BEGAN IN A CHURCH, long before she was at all pretty.

The day was hot—flies seemed to rest on the ladies' hats of tight, delicate straw. No one cried, as if in such heat the salt would be kneaded in. They moaned. But Lucy's voice was light, a ligature to tie the most delicate wound. She sang, "Abide with me, fast falls the eventide."

To her right was the piano, its back facing her so that she saw only the cross-work and the two knobs for movers. Behind it sat Claire, the oldest, and by her on four hymnals stacked in pairs was Josie, the youngest, both dressed, like her, in bleached eyelet.

Because she had seen them seated before she took her own place by the pulpit, she knew what they looked like now. Claire's yellow hair was loosening from the rubber bands, so slowly no one would watch it happen. At first the braids would be tight; they would pull her forehead smooth. By the end of the service, golden tendrils would be curling all around, face set by her—angel for a season of earthquakes. Claire's shoulders curved, the legs stretched for the pedals, and the ties of her ballerina slippers dangled.

In the pinafore, Josie looked especially fat. She swung her legs as Claire played. Then she scowled when Claire threw out her left elbow, jabbing, each time so unexpectedly that Josie would first lean forward to look around Claire's bangs, then turn the page. All the while: Claire inventing little trills on the upper keys. After Josie had pressed open the page with her damp palm, she would try

99

to keep one finger on the new page, try to read the notes. In the rests, Lucy heard the buckles of Josie's sandals hit the bench, out of rhythm.

At the back stood the men, a phalanx, as if their women might escape. Over the oak pews which looked golden, they were dark but for the hands clamped below belt-level and their faces white in the slanting sun. Yet they could fall, like dominoes.

There was the body, her grandfather who now sat at the right hand of God. Below the offertory table was the single rug of royal blue shag, and the casket sat there, open. He looked as they said, pretty. And still, as the body turning silent after a wish.

During the previous week, the children, the wives, the husbands, the grandchildren, the great-grandchildren had come, from Corpus Christi, Abilene, Ft. Lauderdale, Juneau, Los Angeles, Newark, Lafayette. And he had taken each one by a hand, said the names: Joe Junior, Estelle, Myrtle, Franklin, Rebba, Rhett, Peter, Herbert, Mary-Elaine, Lucille, June, Luke, Raymond, Lucy . . . , while, in the front room, they sat and asked, "Hadn't no one not come?"—voices like rising smoke. Food enough for all, clear water in the spring, parking spaces all around the barn and by the woods, everyone's picture at all ages and constitutions stuck in the mirrors. So they gave up, and ate.

When Lucy stepped down, she sat on the front pew, by herself. Rebba leaned forward to say, "Good, Honey, it was plain good," which was a lie. *They* had records of Lily Pons and Rïse Stevens and Marion Anderson. But, not for such discrepancy, Lucy began to cry, softly, into a ruffle, so that, first, what she heard was Jim's uneven walk down the aisle, a sort of hop from the good leg to the bad. And when she looked up, it was to the flash of his Brownie over the casket. Then he limped back. When it was silent, it was like no other silence.

In present time, the church, oddly, is just as it was, probably because, sitting atop the small hill, the graveyard so close you could sit inside and read the inscriptions, there was no room for expansion. No doubt everyone of importance went into Greer to the new church, which had a recreation room in the basement, with moveable vinyl partitions. They allowed guitar accompaniment on Sunday and Wednesday nights.

If one drives by this church, he can imagine no time has elapsed. And, just beyond, sits the Williams' house where once was held a grand reception—white-covered tables filled with red milk glass and blue iridescent figurines and Minton china for twelve.

Of course they put the body into the ground, and, for a long time, he seemed to Lucy to be resting. Claire wore her pinafore the next day as if nothing had happened. Josie stained hers with blackberry wine, the one tiny spoonful each child got to calm him so he wouldn't giggle as he lay next to his cousin on the pallet on the floor. And Lucy finally slept but not before trying to think what to think, her bones hollow as lutes.

But, perhaps, it did not begin there, the eyes opening and the heart seeming to split in two, the breast-bone running between the two, perfect, beating halves where breasts would be one day covering. Before that scene of irresolute stillness, Jim had them out in the Sequoia National Forest, miles from anywhere, in quiet, but for the animals and their own noises, pentangular. Still, Jim had strung four Indian blankets between four trees, for privacy, and, in the middle, sat the picnic table belonging, as it was stamped in red, to the National Park Service, U.S.A. Just beyond the enclosure sat their two trailers made of metal slats, filled with all they owned. Above the boxes and crates and round barrels holding the Wedgewood were two double mattresses laid on two-by-four's. When it was dry, they slept there. Jim said it was good for the lungs, and Pauline, who for years refused to comment on Jim's ideas as if they were a moat she might fall into, said, "Well. . . ."

Even now, the trailers sat without the tarpaulin covers. You could read up there after breakfast, little needles falling on the page, and Jim would walk by, ask, "What is this, the public library?", his arm sweeping out to show Lucy trees and air and sun and, later, the tarantula big as a man's hand.

Claire walked by her as she sat on one of the benches, waiting. She whispered, "If we got bit by a snake, we'd die." But Claire was silly; Jim would make with his pen knife a tiny cross-hatch on the skin, and top the cut with his mouth, and suck and spit. Pauline would put the ice pack over the red and swollen cut. Ice? She would fan it. Look straight at Jim and fan, fan, fan. Times of trouble, Jim would turn to ask, "What're we Americans *for?*" A circling-in.

So it was not the snakes and vermin, the trees dry as hay, the stories about Lodovico as the pines dipped overhead. Josie was in a corner with her bucket and shovel, making a hole. Each time her left arm moved, the blanket shook, which set up a movement through all the blankets. Pauline was at the Coleman stove, set atop the metal grates of the stone fireplace. Claire was filing her nails at the end of the opposite bench. Before her, by the plates, she had put the pink bag holding the red and purple polish, the orange sticks, the remover, and the clippers. Behind her, stretched out on an Army cot, was Jim reading *Variety,* which meant sooner or later they would get to California where he would try out all he knew in his bones, the *pas de deux* of make-believe.

Then the bacon was frying, the smell caught in the enclosure. "Get me some grits, Honey," said Pauline, who always called on Lucy because Lucy's head was never down when she was with them. At the open trunk of the Nash, she stood straight and looked behind her. How deserted! And that, she thought, lifting the edge of the blanket and carrying in the bag, was why Jim put them up. She watched Pauline stirring, then looked into the frying pan. She counted: one, two, three, four, and me, five. She looked out and counted: five, a finger at her chest.

"Is that *all?*" she whispered to Pauline.

"Go sit."

By Jim, at the end of the cot, Lucy stretched her legs before her and put her hands in her lap. Jim turned a page of the paper.

"Lumps," said Pauline. "I poured them in too fast," to no one in particular.

Lucy got up quietly, went to the Nash, to look. There was the food box, and why hadn't she noticed it before: no eggs, a box of salt, container of pepper, corn meal, rice, brown sugar, half a bag of Luzianne, saltines, popcorn, and a box of corn flakes, which she shook—"*Half.*"

At the cot, Lucy sat again, thought. "*Hey.*" Jim poked her hip with a foot.

"*Daddy*"—a hissing—"we're almost out of *food.*" Pauline looked up, waited. But it wasn't at Jim she was looking, who now turned another page. Josie was humming and Claire's tongue curled over her upper lip as she spread the polish.

"Jim?"

"I heard her," he said to Pauline, voice dry. He lowered the paper. "Know what, Little One? Do not *worry.* Remember all the bottles we collected yesterday, which, I remind you, are in the trunk of the Packard? Well, there're literally *millions* of them out there. And, every once in a while, you get lucky, find a crate. Two bucks each. So"—he leaned forward to pat Lucy's head, "don't give it another thought." He shifted, called over to Pauline then— "Listen to this. Says, 'Joel Silverstein of RKO Pictures announced yesterday at the annual. . . .'"

And it was over. Pauline was laughing now and dishing up grits, making in each mountain a little well for bacon grease and putting the plates on the table. Sliding down to sit by a tree where the blanket lifted and fell in the morning breeze, Lucy looked at Pauline, at the face which was still beautiful and at her dark hair, at how she wore earrings even to breakfast. Tiny pearl dots.

It wasn't, Lucy saw suddenly, that they would starve. It was that how they *thought* depended on Pauline.

And would she hold?

Currently, if one goes to visit Jim and Pauline in their separate houses, each unaware of how close the other really is because they have lost touch with one another, it is easy to see that Jim is just as he always was. Every year for years he seems to grow younger, and he is so handsome still it makes the girls at the Save-On where he buys groceries swoon. And his voice, trained, makes them ask sometimes, "Were you ever on T.V.? I think I've seen you on T.V." So he picks his women from among them, so young they can recover, bodies taut and the earthly mysteries like just so many cans of green beans on a conveyor belt.

And Pauline, if the Jehovah's Witnesses come by on a Saturday, park their bikes at the small rise and weave down through the rose bushes, past the willow and the green hose—Pauline opens the door with a look so naked the boys mumble, stick the pamphlets in the screen, slink away and walk their bikes for a mile or two. Pauline, no, she didn't hold, so people who know her story make sure to write to her on special occasions and they pass her around at other holidays, make certain the roof stays shod and the gutters cleaned of leaves.

When Lucy was twelve, a magazine Pauline bought carried a cartoon, which Pauline put each month under Lucy's breakfast plate. A bird, the same bird, pointed a wing straight at whoever was looking and he said, "THIS is a WATCH-BIRD watching YOU." The bird asked such things as, "Have you been mean to you mother?" and, "Do you talk back to your mother?"

But Lucy was never mean, she never talked back. It was the eyes themselves, asking how to cleave. And when Pauline opens the door, it is as if she expects Lucy's eyes, disembodied and mammoth, to settle on the couch.

Sometimes Lucy wanted to talk, as if another's silence could be soft as a hand laid on a cheek or a mouth at the back of the neck, as she imagined, Pauline driving round and round like a dog trying to arrange himself for sleep, Lucy's forehead cool on the glass of the car window, behind Pauline, Josie off, stashed with relatives to keep her untainted, Claire in the front beside Pauline and growing stolid no matter she looked all skin and bones and the hair pale.

She would say. . . .

But, perhaps, it was the Auschwitz photographs from *Life* which in black and white and the incredible shades of grey showed the men, looking like boys but for the eyes and the curling fingers smaller than any boy's, standing transfixed behind the chain link fences, showed the mountains of bodies, limbs sticking straight, naked even of flesh. And, in the text. . . . Then, Lucy began dreaming and waking sore. But awed, too, because, she would want to tell someone, it truly was not necessary to have been there to know how a nerve feels uncovered and how a body can curl until it belongs to no one else, yet, yet—she would grow excited, thinking and learning—they were so close! as, in the dreams, no one moved without another knowing he had moved.

And, dreaming this, in versions for years as if nothing else had ever happened, when they said to her at the reunion, the women pinching her cheeks and patting her thighs from where they sat on benches, turning to each other to smile, saying, "Don't rush it, Honey, because, let me tell you, life isn't all roses," Lucy thought: *That* is what they mean. No matter she moved differently from them.

Out on her own in the world, she thought, as if she were crazy, Really, I shouldn't go into bus stations, train stations, the big stores—where men strolled, as if such privacy as hers were invitational, dangerous as bucking under.

Claire called her now and then. One sunny day she said, "Hey, let's meet for lunch." So they sat across from one another just as sisters might. Lucy liked it, though Claire was growing fat, as if to push all beauty out, a seepage. Still, Claire tossed her head. "Fine, fine," said Lucy. They ordered hamburgers, waited, Claire stirring her coffee and looking up now and then. She sighed, "I don't know. . . ." Then the food came. Claire lifted her hamburger, put it down, lifted it.

She reached to get her sweater, the red-painted nails pausing to tap the table, as if she were distracted. She looked at Lucy, shrugged. "Listen: sorry. I'm not hungry. You're—" and she put on the sweater of yellow and brown stripes, Lucy's hand holding her own hamburger in mid-air. Claire sat, then, quickly, on the edge of the aqua bench. "I don't know. Everything's fine. I got this man I like, he's taking me to Maine next week. Josie's Josie, Momma's fine, so everything's *all right*. But I gotta go." And she was gone, the waitress bringing the check and looking at Claire's back and the closing door.

In time, as if for her relief and as if a storybook opening, a man Lucy liked came along. One look, though you would have argued at such a thing had you read it, the mind working overtime when the body slept. His shoulders curved, the neck dipping forward and the walk as if the calf muscles ached, and so few words all history was in the hand on her cheek. So she laughed, as if the words she *might* say could come tumbling out, which was not necessary at all as he undressed her and she rose to look at herself in the mirror—"Ah, well!", the voice almost booming since she could last forever. And he laughed. When he needed her, oh, she would be there.

In time, he sat her down in a public place where men in dark suits were talking business—so much money, how do they even think of so much money?—and the women in groups, hair done and clothes from Loehmann's, and their children dreamless. Plants hung overhead and the carpet was green as grass in early spring. She ordered Belgian waffles, said to him to have something to say in such a place, "What it means is the indentations are wider and you get a slice of pineapple." She waited. He was sitting straight, he looked tanned.

He said, "This won't be easy: I've got, I don't know, what I figure is six or seven years to be happy."

"*Then* what?" She shifted; the waitress moved away.

He smiled. "I don't think you're supposed to plan 'then what.' It just happens—whatever." He waved a hand.

"So you can't hold me?"

"I knew it wouldn't be easy." Her bones glass and breaking.

Now, if one could see her, she is looking in a mirror, calm, as if that were insouciance itself, for *what?* Except she is thinking how much—which was, wasn't it, a comfort—her grandfather loved her, that he is watching—has never rested!—and is saying to her, "Ah, Bambino, you don't know what hit you or when it will be better."

So, truly, Jim needn't have taken the photographs.

Rock House

BEFORE NINE O'CLOCK the woman had taken down her hair and now, near eleven, was shaking it by the open fire. Her husband had smiled at her, saying she looked like Josie, and she had turned to look at their daughter, then had raised a finger to her lips. The girl was pretending again. The woman wondered if she ever really slept. She thought sometimes, with meanness, that the girl was determined never to sleep so that her parents wouldn't be able to talk, to say anything significant. The woman wanted to call out to the girl, If you're going to pretend, at least stop kicking your legs so I can pretend too. But of course she knew the girl was in a trance, day-dreaming way past dark. Now still kicking.

The man was reading a Max Brand western, his left hand holding the book while his right hand lightly touched the auto-harp on the stool by the chair. She recognized he, too, was in a trance. She almost wanted to play the autoharp herself, a real song, but couldn't bring herself to lean forward and get it. He had bought it for her when there wasn't food in the house and, instead of playing, she became hungry for pecan pie.

Family photographs—his—stood lined across the bookcase. She noticed her hair looked like his grandmother's, and it seemed no time had passed. Above Josie's cot, a baby, photographed in a long, white dress, seemed to be watching. The woman was sure no one would remember the baby if, full-grown, he walked into his family and said he was the same they'd jostled. But then she

107

remembered he wouldn't ever walk in because he was in California where it was warm.

"Whatever happened to Luke?" she asked.

"What?" her husband answered, putting a finger in the book and looking up but past her.

"Luke." She swished her hair around a finger. "I wondered what happened to him."

His eyes focused. "He's fine. In construction, they say. Why?"

The woman looked again at the picture. *She* would recognize him because she wasn't a member of the family. He would look like *her,* the expression, and he would see the similarity too, the way some men recognize some women at cocktail parties and on street corners and in neighborhoods where you walked the dog at night.

"Nothing," she said. "Just wondering." She watched her husband look past her to the newspapers stuffed under the door, his trying to figure if the wind would tear them away before morning.

"Make some popcorn, will you?" He moved his hands from the words and began reading where he left off, or before, or farther on. She pulled her slippers from the hearth and slipped them on as if she were in a shoe store with the salesman watching.

Before going into the kitchen, which was dark and shut off by a door-curtain because the wood stove had gone out, she looked at the girl, trying to decide if they should move her now that the legs had stopped kicking. She hated taking Josie into the other room where the family bed was, the bed the grandfather had died in. She didn't like not having even a hot water bottle with which to warm the bed for her. They said every night as they got in on either side of her, sharing her warmth, that they could have heated some rocks on the fireplace to wrap in towels and given her warmth to go in to. But it was always something they said after the coals had been stirred down, too late.

The man looked up. "Funny. I thought I smelled the corn popping."

She got up, tucking her hair inside the collar of her blouse. "In a minute. White or yellow?" The corn came with the house, theirs now that his father was dead and the mother was in the little house in Greer. He didn't answer, but while she was in the kitchen, reaching up for the wire basket, she heard him call through the curtain, "Luke's son got shot in a poker game." She didn't answer, so he called out, "White or yellow—you decide."

When she brought the basket back and was holding it over the fire, listening, she looked again at the picture. Not him, but someone who *looked* like him. The whole family looked alike; his mother counted heads. She had on her tongue a cluster of warts. It made one notice tongues.

She looked away from the fire. "He died? His boy?"

Her husband tried to pull his eyes from the book; she watched his head moving toward her voice, but then it snapped back. *Of course he died.*

"I wish you'd bring in Sheba."

He didn't look up. "Her fur'd stink."

She shivered. "That was last night, the rain. It's clear tonight, and dry, and almost Easter." The church was nearby, beyond the small house her husband's father had built of wood, one room with a dirt floor where the twelve children had waited while he carried the rock down for the permanent house. And the ladies at the church could not conceive of a woman with one child.

"Bob," she asked softly, "are we going to get out of here soon?" She handed him the wire basket.

He stood, suddenly animated, putting the basket down on the autoharp, which sounded discordant, vibrating underneath. She watched him pull on his red hunting boots, watched him go out, the newspapers scattering, and then listened to him calling for the dog.

She remembered the grape juice the grandfather had put up to ferment. It wasn't done yet but she wasn't dressed for getting high. Those dresses were in the trailer by the shed. Carrying the kerosene lamp high above her head, she almost dropped it when she stepped down to the screened porch. The cabinet shook as she opened it.

Looking at the crystal, she wanted to laugh. The glasses were

dusty from the wagon traffic going past into the woods where the
stills were, wagons carrying either ordinary farmers or women-
haters—she never decided—to their fires. When she wondered
why the grandfather had stood for it on his property, she wished
he'd talked more. And had he picked up one of the real wine
glasses, the Lalique, especially, with a disrobed woman forming
the stem, he might have thought it was a fancy evil such as his wife
purged, speaking in tongues. Yet, in his last week, he had called
out *her* name, had said—a command to his wife—"Let *Irene* sing at
the funeral. I want 'Abide With me,' so everyone will understand."

"They don't *know* her," his wife had whined.

"Well," he had said, "if they *listen* they'll feel like they know
her. Everybody knows her." So she had sung it, *a cappella.*

On the porch, she could hear where her husband had gone, near
one of the stills, and she waited until she heard him coming down
the road, the dog still far off, barking.

"Come have some wine with me," she called, and carried in the
lamp and the glasses, the mason jar of grape juice.

He was reaching above the photographs for the gun, fresh mud
from his boots marking the wood floor. "She's got a rabbit somewhere back of the barn. I'm going after it so we can eat something
decent in the morning." He kicked at the newspapers. "Stuff them
back—this may take a while."

She half-rose. "Wait, let her have some fun chasing it. Have
some wine. We can talk now."

He noticed the jar and stooped down. "Damn, I'd forgotten
this. He did love his wine," he said, laughing to himself as he
unscrewed the lid. "Still not done," and then he sipped. "Good."
He sat in his chair and picked up the book, the suit-coat buttoned
and gapping at the lapels.

She touched her hair, tucking it behind her ears, spreading her
skirt over her knees. "I liked him."

He moved a finger along the page. After a minute he looked up.
"Howard ought to send a letter soon. I sent some tapes of a

broadcast I made when you and Josie were in Anderson. He should write soon. It's a CBS affiliate, so—"—he winked at her—"when the letter comes, I'll get your clothes out and you can go in and have the emerald polished and wear it with the green dress when we go up."

"It's chipped, not scratched," she said. She waited.

Finally she watched him put the book down. "You have to understand," he said, "I'm not taking the job he mentioned. Peanuts stuff, and you know I won't do weather. But, sure, I plan to take you if the network buys. If not, we can just stay here. It's solid, we've got the potatoes, apples, the wine, some corn meal. Momma's got the insurance and one of the others can worry about her for a change if something happens. Shit-Christ."

"Hush," the woman hissed. "Here." She poured more wine into his glass, looking at his hands, white where he held the stem.

"All right," he said, "it's like this: you remember when I did the promo for WZYN? Kentucky?"

She had taken a handful of popcorn into her mouth and now shook her head. She swallowed. "We weren't with you that year, that trip."

"Yeah, right." He propped his feet against the stone fireplace. "You saw the picture, though, and the letter. The Ames Brothers were coming to town. We were supposed to see who could put on the best pre-show build-up. They wrote me a letter, saying 'We sure appreciate all you did,' but I didn't win. Some jerk at WYET. Gave me a silk suit instead, from Hafferty's, because so many people stopped in front of their store where I'd put pictures of me along with pictures of them. I got all manner of letters on that— good for the station and Jim never even mentioned it."

She looked over the photographs on the bookcase, finally finding the one of him and the Ames Brothers, a composite. "You never hear about them anymore—six years ago," she said. "Can't we move with you and not wait?"

He picked up the book and began moving a finger along the page. "That's the wrong one," she said. "You read that one last night." She giggled. "And I'm high!"

"You can't be."

"And I hate Sheba, too. I hate her most of all. Last rabbit, I got the skin and put it on the ledge to dry. She ate it. She's got fur in her stomach. I hope it tickles. I was going to make a purse." She put on a pouty face and turned it toward him.

He dropped his glass, too hard, so that it shattered, and he walked over it and leaned down toward her as he passed. "Cheap."

As the door slammed, she called out, "You look silly going hunting in your silk suit and French cuffs, you know."

Then he was back for the gun, slamming the door again, as she called, "Can't we go with you this time?"

She stood at the door, watching him follow the dog's barking.

Inside, she picked up the glass, throwing each piece one at a time into the fire. She looked around the room, noticing they had forgotten to pull the pages off the calendar, or at least she thought so because one of his sisters had brought down corn meal a few days before, and that must have been Wednesday, mill day. She walked to the calendar and tried to tell what day it was by fingering the pages.

Next to the calendar was a picture of Robert, the one in the Army, his head peeking through the breasts of a dummy woman, one of the joke stills they made up for boys like Robert. *Robert*— she giggled. Two of them named Robert. . . .

She pulled on a sweater and went to the cot where Josie lay. Standing above the girl, she tried to tell if she were sleeping. If she were awake, she'd ask what day it was, maybe Saturday, but now past midnight.

She touched the girl's shoulder, feeling for tightness. She lay beside her, pressing her body into the wood frame of the cot. She listened to the clock ticking and to the sound of the papers moving across the floor. At the funeral, her husband had taken color photographs, the casket open and his father in a suit he'd never worn before. They were stuck on the mirror in the little house in Greer.

She missed him. And why had he built the house of stone, which would outlast them all.

The girl was warm. She touched the hair, soft hair. She began to hum. Outside, under the trees, in their white clothes, or black, the children had argued about the funeral bill. *I,* she said to herself, have not fallen through.

Sometime later, when she was half asleep, she thought she heard voices and she rested on one elbow to listen for her husband and the dog. Nothing moved for minutes and she put her head down again. The girl moaned. The woman listened to the wind and to the clock, to their breathing, and to the sound of her hair under one ear. The lamp went out. Or she had shut her eyes.

And then there were voices again. She felt for her slippers under the cot, wondering where her husband was, if he were talking to someone out there. She tried to stir up the fire, not being able to believe she heard children's voices, wanting light to look with. At the door, she pulled her sweater tightly to her chest and leaned her head out the screen.

A few of the children had on sweaters. But, underneath, their costumes were pastel, crepe-paper-pastel, sleazy material, and, on one of them, a long wash dress which looked like all the sacks the corn meal came in. She counted: twelve.

The girl came to the door, rubbing her eyes. *"Josie,"* the woman hissed, looking at the girl rub her eyes, reddening them—pretending again. And the colors excited the girl, too. She pulled at her mother's sweater. "Can I go? I want to go."

The woman touched her sweater. "Go where?", but not waiting to hear what Josie might say, because of the faces of the children—masks without features. She imagined the eyes underneath—the noses, the mouths, like cut-outs on pumpkins, except, dimly, in her mind's eye, they were etched more clearly, too. And their hands held baskets, filled with marshmallow Easter bunnies, sugary and spotted with plastic grass. She almost reached out to take one, and Josie, too—she could feel the girl's hand loosening from her arm.

There were no sounds, not from the dog or late crickets, no movement at all except from their feet, and she looked down. They were barefooted—boy-feet, small feet, but one pair of Wing Tips such as her husband wore. The girl cried out, "Can we go too?"

"*Hush!*"

The boys were tall, and she had no idea who they were, except that they might be able to tell her what day it was. . . .

They wore crepe paper tunics—light blue. A flashlight the tallest girl carried glowed red at the end. And red was, it seemed, on their hands where, she thought, nail holes poured blood through, enough to stain. Yet their hands couldn't have hurt—they held the baskets tightly, waiting for her to hand out Easter candy.

"What do you want?" she whispered.

"Trick or treat!" they called in unison.

She backed up, pulling Josie with her. "What day is this?" She put one arm around Josie. "What day?"

"Easter trick or treat," the children cried. They held out their baskets, the tallest boy with the shoes pushing his, empty but for grass, into her face.

"I want to go," cried Josie, shoving open the door again.

"No, no . . . I don't think. . . ." the woman mumbled. "What kind of a thing *is* this?"

She felt she might have asked more, but the tallest girl held the flashlight on her face. And then, slowly, she turned its light on her own face, slowly pulling down the mask. "Trick or treat," she whispered. And it was not a young girl at all: the tongue, the warts.

"*You,*" the woman hissed. "Why aren't you in Greer, you're *supposed*. . . . *And who is he?*"—pointing to the boy in the Wing Tips. But of course she knew.

"I won't *have* it."

"Have what?" asked Josie.

The leaves moved. The girl was breathing evenly—pretending, pretending again. And Sheba had gone too far too. No barking, no noise but her own breathing. She smelled the air and knew that it smelled like nothing. No matter what her husband did, it would smell like nothing. She looked at the girl, cast yellow by moonlight, and saw that her legs were not moving.

To herself, she began to hum the grandfather's song, knowing now that whoever listened would know her, after all.

Undersong

. . . we'd rather own this breathing plain of snow. . . .
—Elizabeth Bishop

THE *fussiness* of preparation: chaff, and so it did not surprise Lucy and Faith (whose names, rooted—the lifelong *hearing* of the names which did not lift on the breath, made them seem substantial) when they left the house carrying lists of things to buy—little sails against forgetfulness.

And *their*—Pauline's, Cynthia's, Estelle's—absolute belief that the two would be back in several hours (as they would) with everything *on* the lists purchased and dumped on the twin bed in the room where the raincoats lay.

Pauline, Cynthia, Estelle would sip the lemon tea, play a little piano, wait, without knowing they were waiting; feel the afternoon light shift. Around five o'clock begin to worry, wings ruffling in such boredom—the sixth day, of neither labor nor rest.

The season was indecisive, yet fermenting—around the wood steps a gage of leaves once brilliantly colored. Pauline's house sat in a hollow, a path leading up to the bus stop—the four rooms too small, the house itself hemmed by trees and appearing dwarfed by the two cars as Lucy and Faith turned to look back, Estelle waving from the screened door, a breeze lifting the gauzy curtains of the living room. And memory makes parting impossible.

117

In town, their eyes were sponges (hearts the bins which caught the overflow), so (after the shoe shop, Walgreen's, the cigar store which sold the newspaper from the state capital, Penny's, and the Lebanese carry-out) by the jeweler's window as they looked in at the smoky cube of fashioned stone set in gold curls for a finger just Faith's size, Lucy thought of the fig tree in early spring, before the knot of fruit balloons. The ring, *if* it were for Faith, a seedbed. And she smiled at Faith. "Like it?"

"Oh yes"—the breath long, containing all the longing she could not name. Of course they must buy the ring.

They looked at one another, laughed—rivulets of sound, this purchase a conspiracy—against what? They wouldn't have been able to say.

Everyone was rushing by—the first of winter, presentiment in the wind of snow. And of the imagination of the man turning at the door of Walgreen's, to look at them once and then again, as if he had been nudged, it was truncated. He saw first their socks, red and white striped—the woman and the girl wearing similar socks, as if age made no difference—indeed. Is the woman crazy? And she slouched like a girl, she held her head near the girl's, threw her fanny out, arched her back afterwards. . . . Ah well.

The whole of time, lapping, was before Faith, the braided hair soft and the body a boat. Slowly and by such means as the ring, she would one day be sent out, desire billowing. And memory makes parting impossible.

Later they spilled on the bed all the secondary purchases, the cotton balls and witch hazel, the Schrafft box of chocolate-covered peanuts which they had told Cynthia she should *not* eat, the light bulbs, the red shoes with virgin soles, the jar of pine nuts, one thing and another. "That's it," said Lucy, wadding the lists into a pocket. And, for an instant, she and Faith were triumphant, since (dear, dear Faith) it was not easy to be organized.

"*What* is *that?*", asked Pauline over the bouillon, now that Faith had grown enough accustomed to the ring to forget it momentarily, to lift that hand from her lap and reach for the salt.

"*What,*" asked Cynthia, sniffing, as if, already, Faith were sprinkled with flecked water, gold and silver, and did Cynthia wish on a daughter *that?* Faith's own father awash in another woman's body and Cynthia's bone and fat in cycles rhythmical as the moon's pull.

After the commotion ("How *much?*"—Estelle's eyes squinting—and, "Where? In *town?*"), Estelle, the formalist (when she could remember) now that Carleton was dead and resting, quietly reached beneath the damask cloth to hold Faith's hand. "Thank your aunt," she said softly.

The room became still. It was the kind of stillness before familiar music.

"I did," said Faith, mouth near the fluted collar of her blouse, lips almost buried in the eyelet. Then she looked up and across the white cloth, to Lucy. The eyes said, *Didn't* I? And filled.

"I did."

"Of course you did," said Lucy; then, turning to Pauline, "Pass the rolls around."

There was noise again; even the dog wanted in and scratched at the door. Getting up, Pauline spilled the dish of cranberry sauce, and it was then, as Pauline was rushing to the kitchen for a cloth, that Faith said in a voice bell-pure and resonant as if sounding over miles of snow, "*I thought I did.*"

That far, now, from laughing—the lovely fishes. Ah, in that instant, pushed off. Faith's smooth hair, the bones light, and the veins near the skin of her wrists almost translucent. . . Who, fearful of drowning, would reach her, and, crawling in, how soon love her under the vagaries of sky?

And if blood is thicker than water, thought Lucy, it floats like oil on top. She ate a roll, watching Pauline rubbing salt into the stained cloth, because, really, there was nothing to do. Yet memory makes parting impossible.

And time, of course, passed, though always it seemed like a morning haze over a salt sea, reachable, gentle. She saw Faith at dinners. She saw her father, just after, she imagined, he had had a girl there, the same girl, she thought, as she sat during thunderstorms on his bed and felt the pillow by his pillow, seeing the girl's hair as golden. "Ha," he would say, "your mother hated storms too."

Faith had never seen him. "I'm the most like him," Lucy said. "Same hair, eyes." And Faith, not thinking, had begun to buy identical gifts for Pauline and Jim, so on his table sat the blue bottle in the shape of a violin, on the mantle the same straw flowers, Lucy the deliverer, as he said, "Well that's sweet of her."

Then, over time, as if he had rested enough, Carleton would seem to be at Sunday dinners, Estelle saying, "Pull Carleton's old chair from beside the piano, why don't you?" Or tell a story. It would begin, "Now Faith was just a baby. . . ."

Faith's eyes lowered; Pauline brought out the picture album from which all the ones of Jim had been taken, leaving the four, white, tri-cornered tabs around a space which seemed bottomless.

Faith's head bent to the pages, eyes squinting, learning herself, Carleton, Carleton's dog which now lay at Pauline's feet, sleeping. And Jim, fleshed by absence, any wild thing Faith might conjure true, for Lucy sat nodding, Pauline's red-painted nails held precisely over the empty spots, as if to cover as she explained, "The boat he got from my father, and if you turn the page you can see him painting it. Red, I believe."

And Estelle would laugh. Once she lifted the hem of her church dress to show Faith the red taffeta slip—Carleton's favorite color.

They loved as well as they could. And of that they said nothing, the opened shells white across a long beach.

In time they looked Faith's boys over, sitting them at the head of the table, a succession filling Jim's old place, emptying it, as when he was fermenting and his forgotten cuff-links, scattered, the gage. Estelle liked all the boys. She would ask, "Did Bob's mother get to keep her gall stones or don't they do that anymore?" Or call them by the wrong names, say, "Well what's a body to *do?*" as Lucy watched the table shake, Faith kicking out at Estelle beneath the cloth; watched Faith's new boy look from one set of eyes to another and ask himself would *she*, in time, be like *them.* Of course she would, Faith's fingers now layered with rings, each precious, colors of shell.

Pauline's hair turned from dark brown to almost white; and, some Sunday afternoons while Estelle and Cynthia napped, she would come to stand in the bathroom as Lucy soaked in the tub. She would ask, "Don't you think it needs a tint, or something?", fluffing its new texture and wiping a circle of steam from the mirror. "Whatever, Momma," Lucy would say. "You decide." Stretch her body long in the soft bubbles of the bath, feel her relative youth as shameful, that lie, Cynthia napping in full weight and Estelle colluding with Carleton, their snoring similar, synchronized as oars dipping forward and aft.

Much, much later, when that which had been for Lucy consuming was truly over, and when Faith, sometimes fitful, would be sitting by Lucy on the sofa, painting her nails as Pauline practiced on the piano the hymns for Wednesday choir practice, Lucy would want to lean toward Faith and impart a truth, would want to whisper to her, "Sometimes you can love *more* than you can manage. Believe me, I know." And, as Estelle might, roll her eyes heavenward, a relief, she would be thinking, to join all their mottled pasts with words.

Often, as Lucy drove from Pauline's through the country to Jim's house, with cookies she had smuggled out still warm in the napkin beside her, she would almost forget, she would hand Jim the heavy napkin, laugh as he winked, and then, looking up, see *his* hair in Jim's hair, or *his* hand where Jim held to her arm up the stone steps.

A name is a bouy, she would think, to see me through, as, she remembered, especially when frost was on the ground, she had said his name over and over, *Richard, Richard,* to make the secret rooms he had found *their* room; and he had answered, softly (promise in a calm sea), "Yes, Lucy?"

Oh, we laughed!, she might have whispered to Faith; his body, my body, And why *him?* Three tiny knots along the curve of the spine, the walk itself, and, when a wind blew the pants legs against the calves, where the muscles bunched from so many years of plain, hard work, you see, which, uncovered, *I* saw. . . . Or how one hand can lift: *No, don't talk, not now. . . .*

Sometimes there would be in memory only these sights and sounds, and, taking Faith shopping on Saturdays, holding up against Faith a deep purple sweater, Lucy might think she would see him at any minute, coming from the bookstore, and smiling. She would imagine the three of them stopping on the street, Lucy saying, "Faith, this is *Richard,*" as Faith, knowing her so well, would still herself and look at him, searching, and be proud, then, of Lucy. And afterwards (this blessing), they would all laugh, this loveliness.

Yet, some evenings, when they might be popping corn and, perhaps, because one of Faith's men would be with them in the tiny kitchen with Pauline's apron around his waist though none of them wore one ("Well, he's a man," Pauline would explain)— sometimes when it seemed a room was busiest, Estelle would go to the half-window behind which curtain Pauline stored her sherry, lift the curtain to the darkness outside and look, there, at nothing. And Lucy would feel, then, her own body rising, to join Estelle's visit with the resting, where Richard (*his* theory in the last days) kept Carleton company.

Or Lucy, in bursts of energy as if she might otherwise be swamped, would lie naked with someone other than Richard (how, at first, she thought of it) and feel, instead, Richard's smooth skin, hairless, that surprise his surgeons had made for her which, lifting his white gown, she had discovered, and his hand closing over hers as if to say, "Yes, Lucy?"

And, touching this man who was not him, she would feel his body as shocking and, slowly, in the perversity of desire, turn to him, say another name. *It is not so bad,* she would want to tell Estelle. It is worse than I can say, she would want to tell Faith, for whom death, so far, was nothing at all.

Then Estelle died. "What *of?*" asked Faith, calling from her school and planning to hurry to them. "Nothing, really, I guess. Lonesome, tired," said Lucy, "and there's nothing to do. Pauline's having the dog put to sleep—he can't see now and is bumping into everything, and she thinks it's best." Listened to Faith cry, for Estelle, Carleton, the dog. Sat Faith next to her at Thanksgiving, the table now shoved against the wall so that, still, it would look full. Cynthia said to Faith anybody she wanted to bring home was fine with her, Faith saying, "Thank you, Momma, I will." And for a long time, Estelle rested.

Some days, seemingly most often when it was chilly outside and she had forgotten her sweater, Lucy, taking the trash out to the double green garbage cans sitting beneath the clothesline, would stand still and watch a bird come to sit on the line, watch it swaying back and forth, and almost wait for the dog to bound after it, sending it flying into the trees. She would listen, hear Faith playing the piano or Pauline's violin pulled from beneath the sofa. Hear Pauline banging in the kitchen, or Cynthia, thin now, running a bath. Cynthia might reach up and draw the shade, even though the limbs of a tree dipped low by the window. Or, if it were windy, hear the bird feeder hit against the window sill. Behind the trees, the light would be fading, low across the horizon, pearl-colored. Wrapping her arms close, she would lean against the garage, feel her ribs loosen, the air flowing out.

Then, suddenly, she would miss them, and, picking up the wastebasket, feel her body slowly gathering itself together, and its irritation as she turned to go in.

Near the steps, she might reach out, feel her arm brush her chest where *his* mouth had so often warmed the white, white skin. And, truly, there was nothing to do but go in to be with them, the body full, and drifting.

Descant

HERE IT IS SWELTERING. Claire wears the diaphanous and Josie (I have seen) rolls her shorts to sausages, airs those legs all across town. I fan. I think. Listen to droplets fall from Momma's air conditioner in her lair above the garage. *Gnats should festoon such a love as mine.* He's written on vellum, "How could *my* hard heart matter when love is itself a diamond set in bone?" Which I tell Claire, floating in, saying, *"Rhythmically,* you know, such care, I swear it cools the insides of my arms."

She adjusts her robe, clears her throat, narrows the fleckless eyes: "Fancy." Drifts away.

"Well," I am left to yell, meaning his black stomach-pelt, skin of jewelweed, the incandescent eye. . . . But Claire would take him if she knew, her moods against me a charivari.

So I think counterpoint. "Let's go," I say, "visit Patrick-Marion in the event, later, he gets killed, steps on an open Spam can, severs an artery in a foot, and bleeds to death miles from the front." *I* keep in shape; she looks up horrified. We go.

Wrap Momma up, settle her in the third seat of Poppa's LaSalle left as a memento. And I drive, way up front to keep the stink away; let the chrome winged lady lead me by the hood. I think she wants for not a thing.

Swing by Josie's craft-and-art Emporium, say, "Don't wash, don't tell Ralph 'goodbye' when time is of import." (*"Eat less, eat less,"* My Splendor writes. . . .) So Josie drops her greenware, filters

125

in, and we glide by Ralph belly-to-belly with a jacked-up Ford. *Josie,* I think, *your nights are numbered.*

Don't veer, I tell the seraphim of LaSalle. *The house of My Exquisite is so far from us it would take to get there a leaning in.* Claire and Josie (and Momma wrapped) would, just looking down, want to take a detour by the drugstore for some iodine. Ease out the little rod and mend the scratches on all his leather tomes. Stand his two boys straight, ask, "What do *you* know." Those boys would drown, gold hair floating, chaff of Persephone's mother on a stream.

So we pass Pelzer, Moonville, Anderson Mills, over the tracks of Greer, and down to farmland where bees plumb the clover.

I steer by four-poster hay and the tree of a million rings, Patrick-Marion's bell-less cow of weathered teats. Then Claire and Josie stretch, leg-first against the twilight, sigh, *"Smell* it." When time is impact, Momma left for me.

I lift her up and on passing by give my first love Charlie (when I was a babe) the sweet "hello." And dipping Momma down on the feather bed where Charlie's wife sinks in the farther half, I whisper, *"Me."* Her eyelids flutter. *"Momma,"* I whisper, as Momma's weakest arm descends and disappears. "You two talk," by which I meant (Oh, Stuffed Paramour: *listen*) the nearly-gone can drift together on the tight (I have *no* doubt) raft of bone.

And, in the kitchen, circle with both arms the whole of C.'s rotundity, squeeze, kiss the garland of wrinkles, and soothe his head. "Look," I say, and draw him to the picture-window beyond which Claire and Josie gather the night shawl. "See how their heads tilt toward one another? They are so semi-romantic." I pat my Charlie's heart-bone. *"Feed* us, will you? Hot corn bread and sweet white milk, gherkins from a jar, a tad of butter, some bacon rind, if you have it: I am *starved."* He laughs. (You think, My Lovely, all my men don't know me?) "While *I,* as it were, find Patrick-Marion-Patrick in the barn."

Walk the loved-sick clover, over this little rise and that, under the stars *sostenente.*

"Monseiur," I call to the swinging lantern, "I have come—me, Lucia (whom you last called 'Loo' when we played in the hay)—to say I will knit your feet armours of steel. *Kiss* me."

So he comes, Marion-in-the darkest-eyes, breath making honey and, behind, sweeps of cows' tails to air the way we will be going. "Hi, Honey."

He lifts my blouse, there, and oh, I know the touch is nemesis. I hold his head and all the world's quiet fall on us.

And, in time, I brush his work clothes off, every speck of gold. No beaded eye will see him. (We can dream.) I take his lantern and we go eat, feast-on-feast, you know?

"Your son," I say to Charlie, "will be just fine," and let the faucet flow. He deals the plates, I bring Momma in and prop her up while Josie mashes peas. ("No flight is instant," writes my Mon Ami.) I, I want this house blessed, I want to count the colors in the salt. Touch Marion's knee under a damask cloth.

"Bless," says Claire, digging in across from me. And I look for a long time. *Sister, you are under-defined.* And only Poppa's wildness (I know) made stanchions of those finger from whence music flows.

So I compose while eating: *Love, of the fine linen and the Yale degree:* I am Potiphar's wife *after* the truth hit her belly. Noblesse oblige of hot climates. And if you whimper from the second well, it is not written they will find *you.*

Then Claire plays in the parlour as Marion washes up. I tie the apron strings and cool his neck. "Does she eat?" I ask, pointing to the bed. His eyes fold down; "Ah," and then the moon folds too. I think, by the screen, where the cotton balls puff white as snow against the black relief, how Jesu, Joy of Man's Desiring is Claire's only song. What keeps the body from the heart? How many fatten on a thorn.

When all that can be cleaned is clean, we walk the high night, Claire, Josie, me, Charlie and his favored son. I take his hand, feel the fingers lace. We sing an English round Marion's mother knew, until Charlie finds the salt lick and, rubbing, lays a finger on all our lips. We are comely.

"I hear them crying," Charlie says, and goes to tend the bed. Claire and Josie flatten on the grass; they talk.

I say to Marion, Let's go run. We run! Such meteors against the sky have not been seen. I laugh, a bell against my matted fur. "Put your hand here," I say. "I am lowing." And ("Yes") he feels my throat.

When Charlie swings the lantern, we go in and, lifting Momma up, take the slow roads home.

They sleep.

Craving

. . . now the table replete,
is bigger than the house.
—Elizabeth Bishop

THE DAYS, Annie thought, are like harp string, perfectly aligned, death a night-music weaving; and, when the sun goes down, *Richard* one note, then the tremolo, all the boys, for instance, gone in Korea. What one awaited: caprice among the oboes.

So, as if in syncopation, she would sit straining forward as Quentin drove and Jim talked, silence around them the kettle drum resting.

"You all right?", she would ask her father too often, and Quentin would turn to her in the back seat, shake his head, *no, stop asking him,* and, *Loosen up,* to remind her—*this* to be by the three of them.

True, I said so, she would nod, and settle back.

Yet, nights, in the cabin by the sound, where Quentin had found them, she would wish for Richard—where he touched her, a curling, bones to heat; and, no matter she had not observed the final aspect, death was one white hand on the belly. So why was Quentin gentle now but for his youth, even as he made her body ache. As Jim grew thinner, even as they slept.

Some evenings, at twilight, she would stand to watch them both coming from the pier, their heads like lures bobbing among the dunes; and it seemed important that she stand precisely as she had stood before Quentin came. Jim would tire, stop to rest, and, crouching, sort among the shells, so a part of the ritual of her looking had been that picture, when he stood again, began again. *Sure, the tortoise outwits the hare, so hush and hear him coming.*

The same wind billowed Quentin's jacket as whipped Jim's trousers flat to the puny legs and the shirt across the chest caving in that Quentin did not find shocking—splendid stranger come to bring fish that first evening, the polite knock on the screen door frame. ("Yes, Poppa, I *know* him.") And now they ate fish, not once tiring of fish.

Or of the smell of fish, bones of fish, pictures, talk, exaggerations, and Quentin's almost scientific study of the colorations and swimming-depths and ways of breathing of fish—so much of one thing (Jim in the blue chair, Quentin below him, a step, on the hassock)—if Annie *had* written: *Hurry, Momma, and bring Tina, or you'll be sorry,* it would be as it *should* be if, looking around, sniffing as her eyes narrowed, Pauline had said, "Sheesh!", high-tailing it out; or if Tina, regardless Jim had traded his French cuffs for Quentin's plaid shirts so huge on Jim she might, for once, laugh, said, on listening in, "Not *me,*" and, "You have got to be kidding."

What did Quentin know. *Nothing,* notwithstanding his cool hand on her forehead, her buckling under—suborned by such tenderness.

She would lift her sewing—batiste, white as gulls' wings, embroidered in white, the thread silk-white—and think—looking over at them and, as the Spartan hummed, hurrying.

Tina, she might write to her sister, might have written years ago, *you are perfectly right: our father, as it were, always brought gold and frankincense and myrrh, and such excess from a visitor. . . .*

Mornings, when there was still dew on the scrub plants by the steps and Jim would say, *"Smell* it, Honey," and breathe in, smiling at her for this expansiveness—then, with Quentin behind them both on the incline, as if to catch them, she would see the car, with the sun coming behind it, and almost *become* Tina, eyes rolling heavenward: this pure idea, squat on the top of the dune. *What is the use, hunkering.* And then Annie would feel herself stiffen, so she might fall, and that was what Quentin was for—such moments when he would say, "So where to today?"

Voice, a bird on the wing.

Yes, Jim would have bought a Fiat, black, with silver. After which the boys from the pier would have ambled over, one swinging his legs over the side, cocking his head as the right hand rested on the leather-covered steering wheel. He would say to Jim, "Can I give you a lift?", tongue savoring. And Jim would call to her, "So what does The Lady think?" Then all she could imagine possible would be the lifting of her fluted collar to her lips, its falling once, and, *"Je ne parle pas français, Monsieur."* To watch the boy shrink, as he should.

And the boy might have been Quentin—the tall one whose fantastic hair was bleached coral. And Quentin had not been with her, to advise, politeness honed. She had found, on her own, the Nash Ambassador, 1949— Quentin *whistling* when he saw it. . . .

Had it painted the same ash-blue from which time and shade Jim could recall Yosemite and the hot springs, natural bridges of Arizona; Tina, then, hardly mean at all, Pauline thin, also a receded landscape. He could walk around it saying, "I'll be damned," and, across the hood, ask, "You're something else, you know that?", forgetting (she would blow him a kiss) how the back seat lowered into a bed for the weary.

"We are now passing," she had called out to him, "the Royal Hart Motel where you taught me and Tina shuffleboard," and, "There's The 'Bott'ry,' as Momma said," to make, again, his two girls flutter, Pauline a calm sky.

And now she leaned forward, her head resting on her crossed arms, one hand near Jim's shoulder as she looked at him, the neck skin in folds and, for that, the nose seemingly straighter yet, of the undocumented aristocracy. They seldom touched, not even this hand to his shirt.

"You know the Pawley Island Hammocks? We should get one."

And Quentin waited at the wheel, the pure state, because he did not know the picture—Pauline's back yard, its trees dense, weeds overgrown, the hammock there over the grassy spot, and if you watched from the back window, you saw, when the wind blew, both movements, of the rope and the grass and, then, above, the bird house swinging on a wire.

But her father laughed, he lit a Camel. "Nah, Honey, I saw one the other day—they use half the rope they used to. Japanese rope."

So all of it was done now, was it. "Well anywhere, Quentin."

Tina and Pauline inside with the air conditioner; if she wrote to them even in the stringent surveyor's language, they would read it there, the dropped line, the eye, and the sun unimaginable.

Possibly, Tina, excess calms the nerves. How Richard thrashed near the end! Friends had told her so. Then he had smiled, she *knew*.

With Quentin in charge now, the car filled with cans of soft drinks, and the beer Jim liked stowed in the cooler, sardines and pâté de fois gras and Waverly crackers in a paper bag; the boots, coated in yellow rubber for the times he would stop the car near an inlet into which they would wade to fish as she sat, mending, now, their wool socks.

And, even, in time, she traded the paper bags for a hamper, a flowered table cloth, napkins to match the cloth.

"Class, huh?", Jim would say to Quentin, winking and shaking a napkin, a flourish, and a picture as he tucked it under his chin, smiling at her.

"*Up*bringing," she would answer, and laugh until they laughed with her, this autumn turning, lovely, and slow.

As the winds grew colder, they went less often to the pier, her watching as they returned relinquished to the weather. And, with the jalousied windows closed, the house seemed to shrink—the bedrooms, low-ceilinged and tiny. But, more, how *visible* each object they had brought with them, Quentin's still new to her, though it had been months, and she would find herself stopped in the hall between their rooms, looking into his, at a jacket thrown across a chair. And it seemed then to belong to no one. If she passed him and he looked up, he would ask, seeing her eyes, "What's the matter?" If she could *name* it, well, then. . . . And, those moments, she would want to touch his hair, her hands gentle, all that they had accumulated for this time-of-times pointless.

So, too, she would often stand at the door of Jim's room as he slept and watch him, or, watch the shape on his bed, the curve his body and the blankets made; the sound of his quiet breathing and, coming in swells, of his teeth grinding, body caught against a dream. And she would wait there until he breathed evenly again. His room appeared to her spare, as it should, she thought, although she picked the last of the wild flowers, put them in jars on the table and chest.

Sometimes Quentin would read aloud to Jim, who might laugh and say, "Too deep for *me*," but, more often now it was Jim's voice—quiet, as if not to disturb her—she came to listen for if she had been out walking and stood, gauging, at the doorway.

And it was as if Jim had suddenly *discovered* Quentin, who

nodded: how the Rockefellers managed their money or how Jefferson had loved the very skin of his, as Jim would say, "octoroon" mistress—these facts Pauline had felt as a swarm of bees around her.

"He's great!", Quentin would say to her in the kitchen, and he might, then, touch her breasts with the cold glass he held— "Want one?", because they had begun, too, buying Wild Turkey, to accompany Jim's beer.

"Well," she might say to her father, bringing in a tray with tea and sugar and the lemons sliced paper-thin, "tell me about Granddaddy, given I barely knew him," her voice booming, making her shiver.

Jim would have his Wing Tips off and paired by the hassock. He would take his time answering, as if her voice came from within a shell. Then, "What's to say?" Shrug.

"Well?", hearing her voice rising: *You all don't know a thing about time,* at which a picture of the three of them—Pauline, Tina, Jim—would flash once, and they would appear standing in front of a drug store, arguing over nothing at all as their ice cream cones dripped; Quentin at her side, waiting, though he had not yet been born.

He would put a finger to the page of the book Quentin had given him, smile at her—indulgence. "Well you know, Honey, a farmer. Sold insurance on the side. I took him back to his old home place before he died. We drove up on a Saturday, stayed at a Howard Johnson's—he'd never been in one. There wasn't much left of his house, of course. But, what-the-hell, it was what he wanted."

"You did that?"

"Well sure."

And Quentin would look at them, from one to another.

Mornings, the car was layered in frost, so they began to sleep late, to awaken after the porch was warmed and to sit for a time with the newspaper, brought by the brother, Jim explained, of a girl at the Kroger Save-On, which girl Annie pictured as she leafed through the paper, who would wear Chartreuse cologne.

"*Are* you all right?", Annie would ask him as she poured him coffee, her arms, she imagined, flecked here and there with bits of shell.

"Sure, Sweets, and how 'bout you?"—this lovely day, sky powdery. . . .

"Poppa?", she asked. "Do you want to go home?"

"No, Honey, it'll keep."

And Quentin still asleep. Pauline, Tina, (Richard), sleeping.

"Stay with me through the night," she asked Quentin, because, now, she did not want to watch him turn at her door, the clothes he held bunched in front of him, or hear the sound as he dropped them on the chair.

Now she listened to him sleep beside her—so quietly!—after he had held her and had, on going into her, said the two words, "How's this?"

A rubato.

And she did not wish for Richard.

Of course: Pauline and Tina would not have come to be with them.

So, then, it could be said Annie knew, bone against bone, that Jim would begin to go to the dance hall beyond the pier, although much later, when Quentin *had* made her laugh beneath and above and around him, so much playing Richard would have smiled, remembering her—even then *she* would not have *said* so—Poppa! *Words?*, this gift, from Quentin.

Who would wait for a time after Jim had said, smiling, "Think I'm out of cigarettes," and, after Jim had left, car keys jingling, look at Annie, say, "I'll go see." And she would watch him walking on the ridge to the lights beyond the pier.

"What does he *do?*", she whispered after the first night, when she was still cold from having watched on the steps for so long.

"Well, nothing," said Quentin. "He dances," and, "It's all right." And, later, when she wanted to get up, to go again to stand at the doorway of Jim's room, Quentin said, *"No,"* touching her belly. "Go to sleep now."

And, as it was, when she did go to watch, to stand in the doorway of the dance hall, her hand stamped "Luna's" so that, they explained, she could come and go, it was as much to see Quentin in such a place as Jim, whose head was resting in the girl's hair as they swayed—in such light the girl need never know, when he laughed, how many teeth were gold-filled and how many missing, or how, mornings, he limped on one leg until that leg warmed. His hands rode at her waist, hers closed together at his neck, and, in her ear, all of the sweet things Pauline had once loved.

But, of Quentin, she did not so much watch as feel his stillness as he leaned against a wall, so much of himself observing Jim that he would not have imagined the true excess of looking for her, *Annie,* the youngest.

Tina, there is nothing to say.

If, then, Annie was startled when the girl from Luna's came the first day of full sun, with her brother and with her own two boys—little "accidents", she called them, laughing to make Jim laugh as she fluffed her hair and gave him her arm after he rounded the car—if Annie did not see, at first, the cake, so that the girl said, "Chiffon, *lemon* chiffon—everybody likes it"—or think, until later, how like Quentin it was to take the cake from her and, lifting the cover, smell it, savoring—it was, she could say, the sun, the residue, a silt.

Because the house seemed crowded, Quentin took her walking, by the water, where she had not gone during the coldest months. From there she looked up and saw the cabin, every room lighted, Jim's girl moving between the kitchen and Jim's chair, the sound of the boys' playing sometimes audible when the wind died down. Once she thought she heard Jim laugh, and the girl's, answering, and she looked up at Quentin, rolling her eyes as Tina might. She sighed.

Quentin stopped her then, one hand holding her face still. "You're *shy*," he said.

"I worry that. . . ."

"And it will pass," he said.

Printed May 1982 in Santa Barbara & Ann Arbor
for the Black Sparrow Press by Graham Mackintosh &
Edwards Brothers Inc. Design by Barbara Martin. This
edition is published in paper wrappers; there are 300 cloth
trade copies; 200 hardcover copies have been numbered &
signed by the author; & 26 lettered copies have been
handbound in boards by Earle Gray & are signed by
Eve Shelnutt.

Eve Shelnutt, who teaches in the M.F.A. Writing Program at the University of Pittsburgh, was born in Spartanburg, South Carolina. She received her B.A. degree from the University of Cincinnati and, in 1973, her M.F.A. from the University of North Carolina at Greensboro, under the auspices of the Randall Jarrell Fellowship. Her first short story won the Mademoiselle Fiction Award and, since then, she has published stories in many literary journals, including *Ohio Review, Ploughshares* and the *Virginia Quarterly Review*. One of her stories appeared in an *O. Henry Prize Collection* and was reprinted in the Bantam anthology *Stories of the Modern South. The Love Child* (Black Sparrow, 1979), Eve Shelnutt's first published book, was awarded the Great Lakes Fiction Award in 1980.